THE FULLNESS OF
Joy

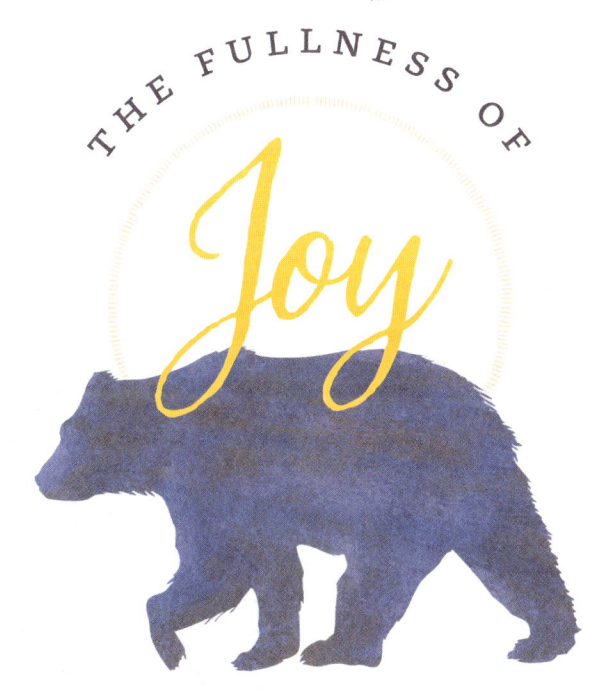

Georgia Briggs

ANCIENT FAITH
PUBLISHING

CHESTERTON, INDIANA

This book is dedicated to Ruth, Nika, Natalia, Francis, and Seraphina.

The Fullness of Joy
Text and illustrations copyright © 2022 Georgia Briggs
Hand pencil drawings: Georgia Briggs
Finisher and colorist: Amber Schley Iragui
Author photo credit: Laura Fecanin
Cover art: Amber Schley Iragui
Scripture quotations are taken from the King James Version.
All rights reserved.
No part of this publication may be reproduced by any means, electronic, mechanical, photocopying, recording, scanning, or otherwise, without the prior written permission of the publisher.

Ancient Faith Publishing
A division of Ancient Faith Ministries
PO Box 748 • Chesterton, IN 46304

store.ancientfaith.com

ISBN: 978-1-955890-08-3

Library of Congress Control Number: 2022938129

PRINTED IN THE UNITED STATES OF AMERICA

*"And if the book will be
too difficult for grown-ups,
then you write it for children."*

—MADELEINE L'ENGLE

This is the story of a bear.

To tell the story of the saint would be too difficult and too important a task, so we shall instead tell the story of the bear, which itself has so much sorrow and joy that we fear we are unequal to this task as well.

But no one else will tell her story, for she is just a bear.

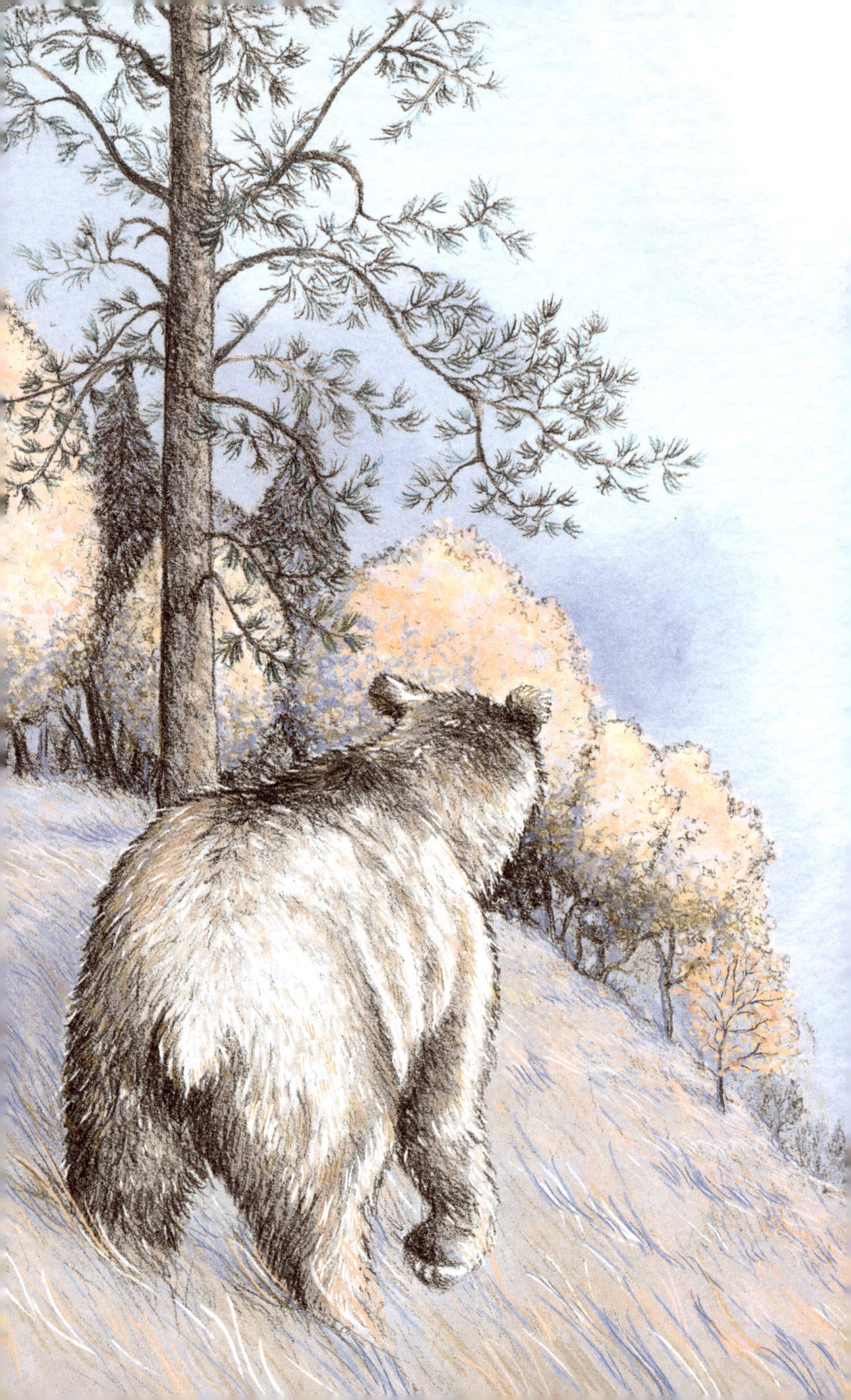

CHAPTER ONE

The call came in late summer, when the sunlight changed from orange to white, and the first cool wind bowed the tops of the pines into prostrations toward the great river.

The bear raised her head and looked north.

She had no name, for bears do not keep names unless they are given one by a son of Adam. They have an ancient memory that Man was made name-giver by the Great Master when the earth was still a cub.

She was like any other bear in the wilderness of Russia. You may picture her standing on all fours in the thicket—the ridges of her brown ears and back shining amber in the sun, her snout slightly crooked, her brows slanted upward over dark, sad eyes.

She had just passed her tenth spring with no cub.

Two fox kits poked their heads out of a nearby hole, saw her, and disappeared again, yipping.

The bear seemed not to hear them.

Everywhere in the forest there were young creatures—wolf cubs tussling, fawns hobbling on stilt legs, baby rabbits poking quivering noses from their warrens, nests overflowing with cheeping balls of down, and *cubs*—beautiful, sweet, round bear cubs with dark, shining eyes and tiny, perfect paws, always fiercely guarded by their mothers.

The bear could barely stand to see a cub, her longing for one was so strong.

You may not see it, watching her in the thicket, but there was a deep hole inside her. She could feel it. It was a dark, painful emptiness inside her womb. Every year it grew larger.

Of course, she was only a bear, so she couldn't express this great pain. She didn't even fully understand its cause.

But now, on this day when the world stood at the highest peak of summer and leaned toward autumn, she sensed something in the north.

CHAPTER ONE · 9

She left the fox cubs still yipping and began to walk.

Humans want a destination for their journeys, but the bear needed none. She walked long. She walked alone. To her, life was much the same as before. Only now she was moving.

Every day she went as far as her legs could carry her, stopping only to eat leaves and berries. She didn't have the spirit to hunt. When she was too tired to walk farther, she would lie down in the open. She found that she slept better with sore paws and weary muscles to keep her mind from the dark void inside.

For this reason, if no other, the journey north was enough of a destination in and of itself. The effort brought her some relief. If she didn't understand what she was fleeing or what she was seeking, did it really matter? Maybe to a human, but not to a bear. She might have continued on forever this way.

But she did have a destination, even if she herself didn't know it.

She walked until the leaves fell and crunched under her enormous paws. She walked until the other bears were swaddled in warm fat and sound asleep in their dens. She walked until the first white flakes fell and covered the ground.

Sometimes she heard the jingle of a troika in the distance or saw a village with smoking chimneys in the valleys below.

Sometimes she was the only living thing in a wilderness of white.

The snowy plains gave way to a forest of green firs. She continued resolutely, weaving through the trees, blinking when the needles stung her eyes and snagged her matted coat.

One day, the trees parted, and the bear stopped. She waited for the dark hole inside her to throb, as it did whenever she was still, but nothing happened.

She stood in a little clearing, only a few meters away from a snow-covered cabin built of wooden boards. A glimmer by the door caught her eye. A tin plate lay in

CHAPTER ONE • 13

a spot of sunlight, piled high with scraps of something brown and soft-looking.

A sparrow landed next to the plate. It pecked at a crumb cautiously, then hopped closer.

Two waxwings watching in a nearby tree fluttered down and tussled over the biggest piece.

The bear was hungry. It was past time to hibernate, but on her journey she had gained none of the warm cushioning she needed to sleep through the cold months. Keeping an eye on the cabin, she lumbered forward.

The birds retreated to nearby branches.

The bear ignored them. She sniffed the brown stuff. It smelled like no food she'd ever tasted. Her mouth watered. She took a bite.

Is it possible to taste love?

The brown stuff tasted like love, the bear thought.

She ate ravenously while the birds fussed at her from the safety of the trees. Soon she was licking the remaining crumbs from the plate with her long pink tongue.

The tin was so shiny she could see her own black nose and the blue sky. And something else. The bear looked up.

The cabin door had opened. Standing before her was a

little man robed in linen, with a silver beard and twinkling eyes. "The birds will not stop shouting about the robber who has taken all the bread," he said, a smile peeking through the beard. He looked up and called to the waxwings. "Here, calm down, my friends. Our visitor was hungry, and you are nearly too plump to fly!"

The birds instantly quieted. The sparrow reappeared to land on the man's shoulder, its tiny yellow claws digging into his robe.

The bear did not move. She felt she ought to run, but the same pull that had tugged her north kept her feet planted on either side of the empty plate.

"There. That's better," said the man to the birds. He held out a hand to the bear.

She sniffed his fingers, keeping an eye on his face. He smelled of the brown stuff and also of something tingly and spicy, like the oil of pine needles.

He slowly moved closer to pet the bear's great head. "Christ is risen, my Joy."

She closed her eyes in contentment.

"Now I'd better find something else for you fellows to eat," he said to the jays.

The bear sat down in the snow and waited patiently as

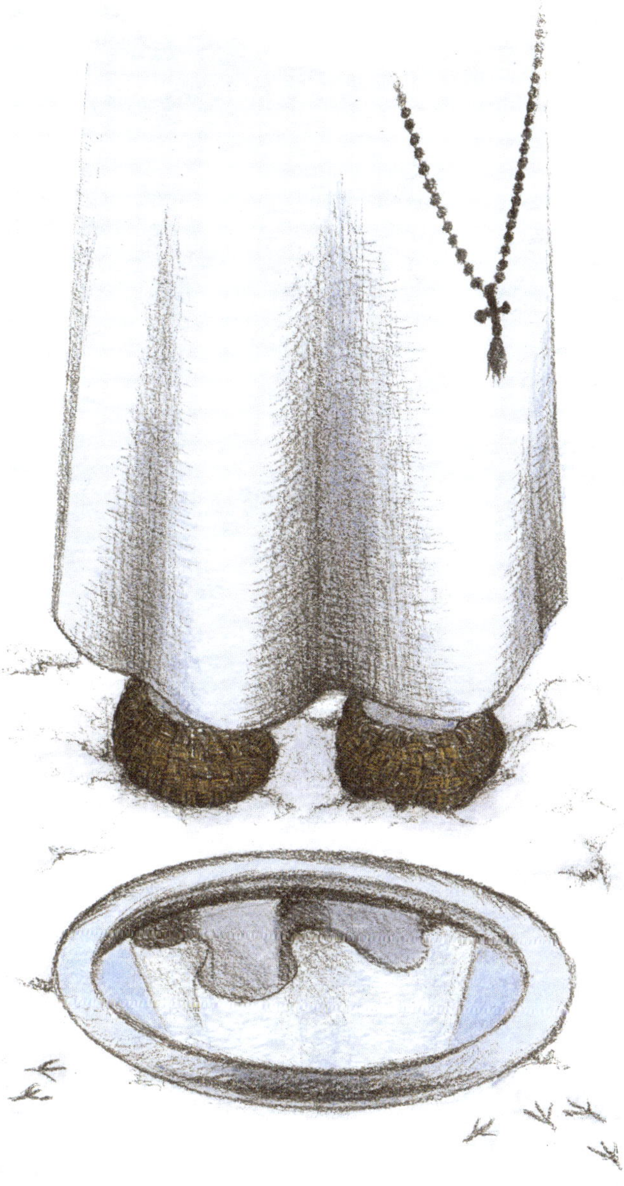

he shuffled back into the cabin. She knew her wandering was done. He had called her Joy. She was named.

She was not the only animal to visit the man. Squirrels and chipmunks came, lynx and martens, birds of all kinds, and even an old bull moose with antlers large enough to make her nervous. None, Joy thought privately, loved him as much as she did.

She gave up any idea of hibernating for the winter and made her den in one of the caves nearby. Every morning she woke at sunrise, fished in the river, and made her way to the clearing to see the man and eat more brown stuff. *Bread*, he called it. He nearly always had a crust of it hidden somewhere on his person, in a pocket or a sleeve of his robe.

He was a strange one. Each day he fed the animals and got to work, singing to himself as he went about tasks Joy could never understand. At first he would go to a little cave near her den, where he had placed a wooden box filled with straw. There was a picture of a human woman and her baby inside the box, and the man would stand in front of it and sing the same songs every day.

Joy crammed herself uncomfortably into the cave behind him and tried to watch the picture of the woman

CHAPTER ONE · 17

and baby with the same fervor as the man.

"Glory be to God in the highest! And on earth peace, goodwill toward man!" he sang.

The emptiness in Joy's womb ached a little as she looked at the mother and the baby.

The man stopped singing and turned to look at her.

She tried to be very still in case she had disturbed him somehow.

"It is hard for you," was all he said. He laid a hand comfortingly on the side of her face. How did he understand?

He turned back and started to sing again, a slower, sadder melody. *"From my youth, many passions have fought against me... but do Thou help me, and save me O my Savior...."*

Joy stared again at the mother and child. The mother's eyes looked sorrowful, even as her baby pressed his forehead to her cheek.

The bear lay down on the cold stone and rested her muzzle on her paws. She would stay here with the man and the sad mother who somehow knew how she felt.

After the cave with the box of straw, the man went back and forth between two of the tallest hills in the forest. At first he would sing *"Blessed are those who are hungry, for they shall be filled!"*

Joy was beginning to understand his words—not their individual meanings, but the feeling in them, as though his earnestness cut through the jumble of sounds and spoke to her in a shared language.

She thought the song about the hungry being filled was nice; clearly it was about the bread that came out of his pocket whenever she nosed his palm. No matter how much he had given already, there was always more somewhere. She often stalled on the first hill, pestering him for more bread, and dragged her feet sulkily when it was time to leave.

He would start down the hill with or without her, and eventually she'd follow.

They would climb the second hill together in the latter part of the day. This one was taller by far, and the man seemed to struggle with his legs, which were swollen and unsteady. Joy walked slowly beside him, even though she could have reached the crest in a few long bounds.

"Thank you, my Joy," he would say, resting a hand on her shoulder for support.

She would blink in a dignified way, thinking disparaging thoughts about the bull moose, who could have carried the old man on his back if he cared to do so.

Joy could have too, of course, but this never occurred to her.

At the top of the hill he put another picture, this one of a man standing on a mountain inside a blue egg like a robin's, hands outstretched. They would lie in the snow face down in front of the picture, just as the tiny painted men lay before the man in the painting. Joy usually took a light nap since the old man stayed motionless for so long. She woke up grumpy when it was time to leave, and stalled here as well.

Last of all was the garden. Not a real garden, but a little quiet place where the man had built a stone wall and wooden bench. Here he would come to weep. He would kneel and put his head on the bench. He had a brass cross on a chain about his neck, and he would squeeze it tightly in one hand as he prayed. The tears would come eventually, making dark blots on the rough wood.

Joy, being a bear, could not weep with him. But she did what she could. She remembered the sad mother holding her baby, and she turned her thoughts to the painful emptiness of *no cub*.

They sat together in that place that always seemed colder and darker than the rest of the forest. None of the other creatures followed him there.

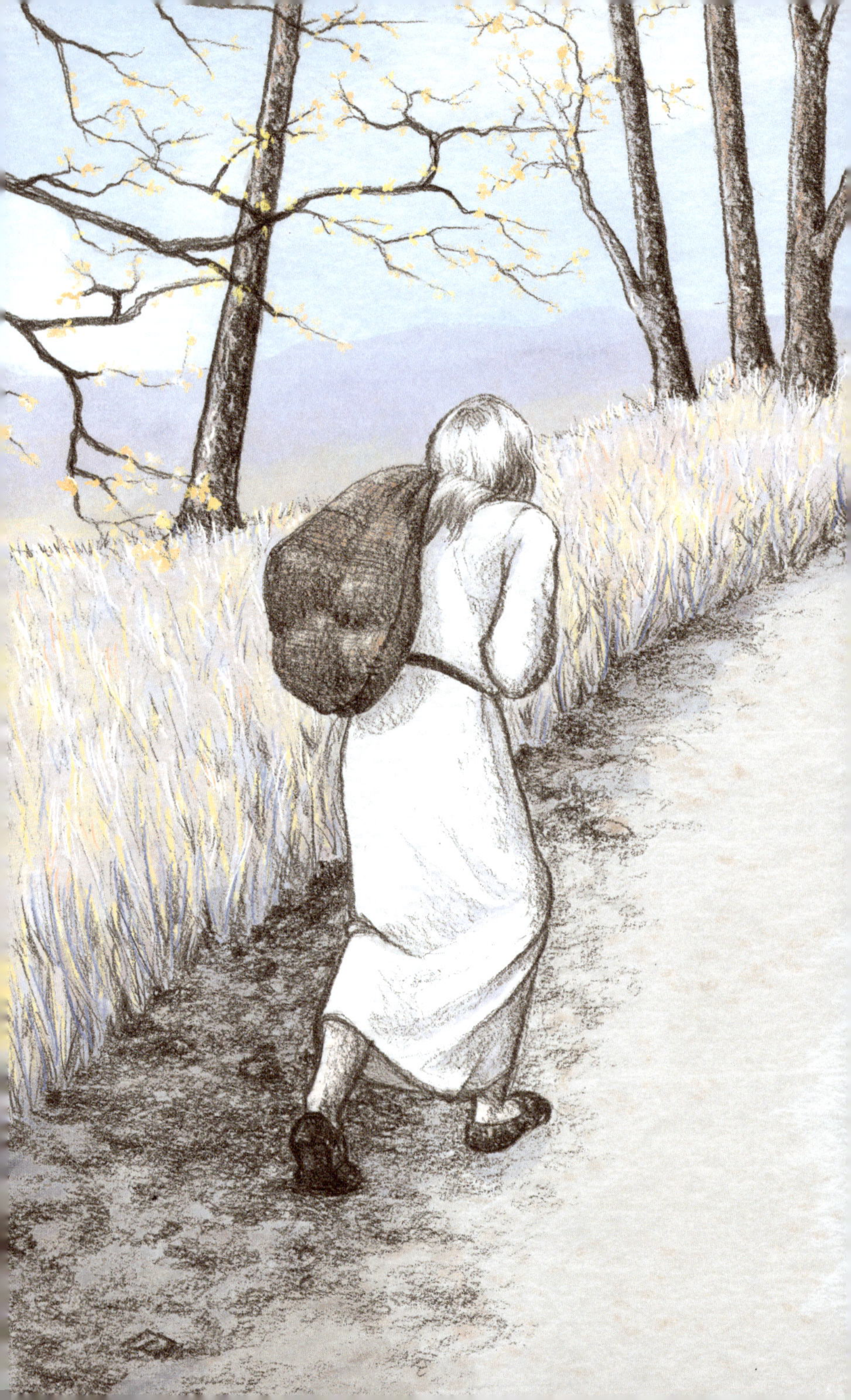

CHAPTER TWO

Once a week the man left the cabin and walked three miles to a great cluster of man dwellings outside the forest. Joy would follow him each time to the edge of the trees, then watch him as he left her to rejoin the black-robed men who were always waiting.

The first time, she was frightened when one of the men pointed at her and began shouting.

"*Batiushka!*" he cried. "Look out behind you! A bear!"

"Hush, hush! You'll frighten her," said the old man. He turned and waved to Joy to show her everything was all right.

She sniffed. She had no idea how he could stand these loud, needy people.

The man would stay overnight at the man dwellings then return the next day with a sack full of bread, looking cheerful but tired.

Joy hated it when he did this. The men were loud, whining cubs, but without any of a cub's endearing qualities. Why couldn't they take care of themselves? Batiushka, Batiushka. They were always asking for more of him.

She put up with it because she had to, and anyway, without these trips there would be no more bread. The only part of his absence she looked forward to was the sound of the bells ringing on the evenings and mornings he was gone. Joy thought the sound was like honey.

Somehow all the animals knew when it was time for Batiushka to return. Before he even came into view, Joy heard the rustle of tree branches as birds and squirrels gathered, and she smelled the old fox in the shadows. The others spoiled their reunion, and she often growled and nipped at them to try and scare them off, but they paid her no heed. She felt the creatures' restlessness on all sides as Batiushka waved goodbye to the men and turned his face to the woods.

She had no words, being a bear, but there was a distinct sense of *my turn* in her satisfied look when

CHAPTER TWO · 25

Batiushka entered the shadow of the trees.

Winter eased into spring. The snows melted, sending trickles of water down the rock wall of the cave where they sang to the picture in the box of straw. Joy's winter coat fell out in wispy tendrils that floated like ghosts around the clearing. Batiushka began breaking up the earth beside the cabin with a metal spade, working till sweat stained the back of his white robe. He sang while he worked, too. He was almost always singing, unless he dropped into one of his strange still-spells, when he leaned on the spade and stared off into the distance.

Joy never bothered him when this happened. She stood near and gazed in whatever direction he happened to be facing, enjoying the warm sunlight on her back and letting her mind wander.

It was the first spring she had not waited anxiously to see if a cub was on the way. She had Batiushka to look after now.

The humans were a nuisance. Groups of peasants had begun showing up at the cabin to speak with the hermit, and Joy was grumpy whenever she had to make herself scarce to avoid frightening someone. She thought she could sense Batiushka becoming frustrated with the interruptions as well. How could they do their work in peace with people coming around at all hours? Joy didn't care about whom they married or which job they took, or any of their trivial concerns.

They had no respect for him. Couldn't they see he was doing important things?

She didn't actually know what he was doing, scrabbling around in the earth every day, but she was certain it was important. At first she helped him turn over the earth with her claws, and even pulled out roots and stumps for him from time to time. It turned out to be hot, unpleasant work, so she decided instead to stand guard over the little garden to make sure the birds didn't eat the seeds tucked into the soil.

Birds and men were so much alike, Joy thought. They showed up and made a great deal of noise and fuss until

Batiushka fed them, and then they disappeared until they needed him again. She was glad he had someone like her to take care of him.

One terrible day in late spring, a man came to visit the hermit and *did not intend to leave.* Joy noticed the sack of clothes and books the visitor carried with him, but thought nothing of it until she returned from a scavenging trip to find Batiushka sitting on the rock in the clearing, still listening to him, and the sun almost set. She waited in the trees for the visitor to leave, but he talked on and on about his admiration for the old man, his longing for the ascetic life, and his frustration with his brothers who had so little ambition.

"Come in, it grows dark," Batiushka said finally. He got up to go open the door for the man, and Joy almost

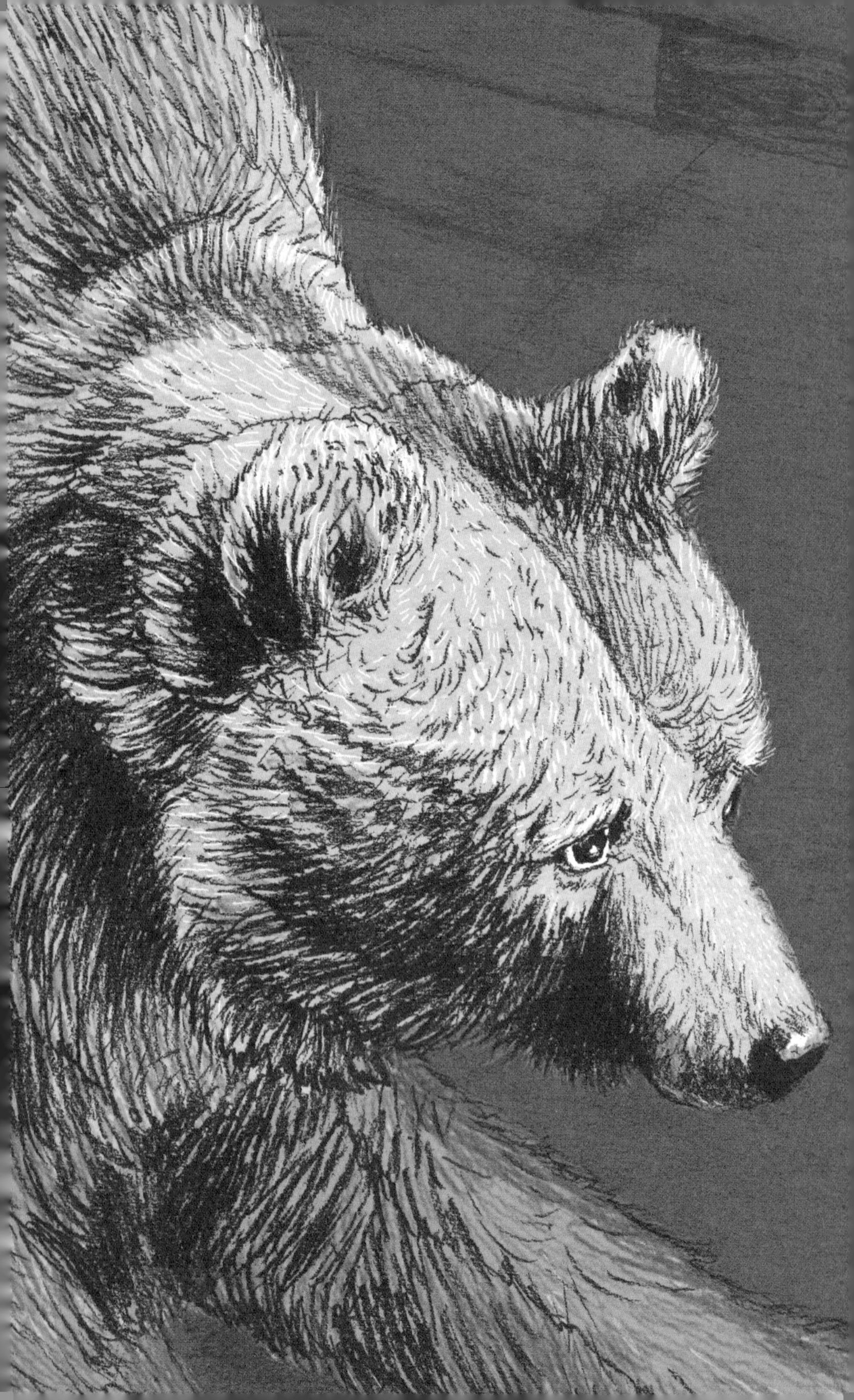

thought he smiled in her direction. But he couldn't have seen her.

"Oh," the man said, "what a quaint little cabin. It's such a relief to live in a place of simplicity at last." The door closed behind him.

Joy came out of the trees and went to lie down beneath the window. She was anxious at the disruption of their routine, and she didn't feel right going back to her den and leaving the old man with this stranger.

"You may have the bed, and I'll sleep on the floor." Batiushka's voice floated through the chinks in the wall.

"Oh, Batiushka, I couldn't take your bed!"

"It's the river's bed, not mine."

Joy could hear the laughter in the old man's voice, but didn't understand his words.

A moment later there was a cry of discomfort. "Father, what is in this mattress?"

"Only the smoothest stones," said Batiushka. "The rough waters have worn down all their sharp edges. Now they can wear away yours."

The visitor was quiet. The cabin was silent for such a long time that Joy almost fell asleep. The night was warm and comfortable.

A rustling from inside stirred her.

"You can't sleep?" came Batiushka's voice. "You'll be very tired tomorrow if you don't get your rest."

"I can't sleep in your bed, Batiushka," said the visitor. He sounded embarrassed.

"Take the floor then," the old man said kindly. "It's better for the back, at any rate."

There was more rustling and the click-clack of stones shifting as they changed places. Soon Joy heard Batiushka snoring softly.

"I believe I should pray some more before taking such a large step," said the man in the morning. He cast a nervous glance at Joy, who was irritable with him and hadn't bothered to hide.

"Undoubtedly a wise precaution," said Batiushka. "It is never prudent to lift heavier burdens than those God has given us."

The man looked sad as he walked down the path back to the monastery, shoulders bowed and head down.

Joy chuffed into Batiushka's palm, and he searched in his pockets for some bread to give her.

"You are not sad, are you, my Joy?" he asked her.

She crunched the stale bread with unnecessary vigor

as they watched the man disappear.

"Now, there's no need for spite," the hermit said quietly. "When you are truly full of goodness, you'll see the good in others as well."

She was still not sorry to see the man gone.

"It would have been too much for him. Things are about to become harder," said Batiushka.

Joy, who slept on stone every night, was not worried.

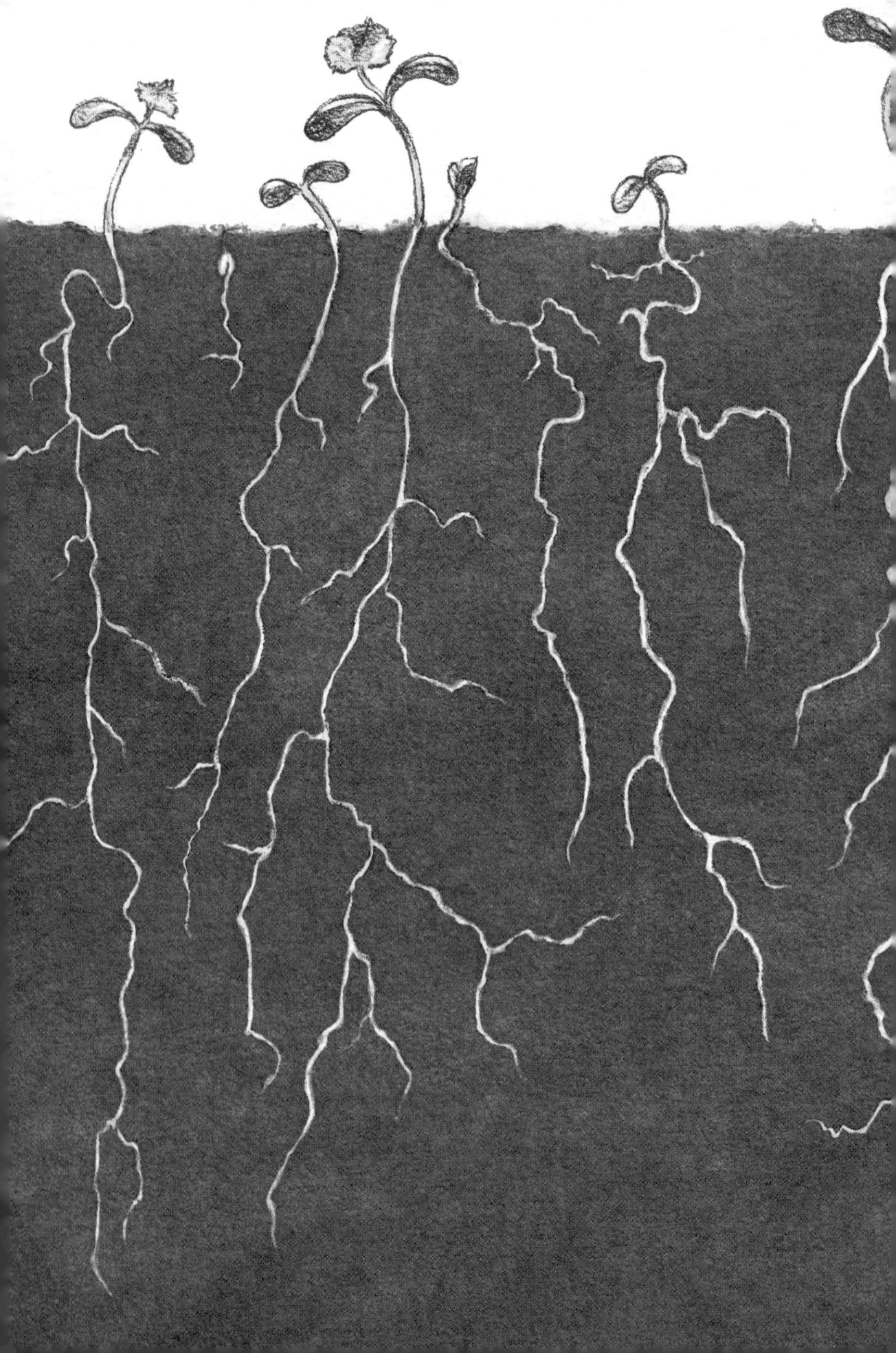

CHAPTER THREE

At first it seemed like Batiushka's prediction had been wrong.

Joy found herself amidst the sweetest time of all her life. It was full summer in the wood, and she had almost forgotten about cubs and darkness in the constant company of the hermit. The seeds he had planted in spring became little green shoots, then leafy sprigs, and now drooped under the weight of vegetables.

The bear was amazed. What wonderful power Batiushka had, that the earth itself would make food at his command.

Fat, fuzzy bees visited the garden, glowing yellow in the sunlight. Joy followed them back to their hive and helped herself to some honeycomb, which she took back to Batiushka. He put it on their bread (what incredible ideas the man had!) and they ate it in the evening when the work was done.

Work was sweet, prayers were sweet, and the silence between them was like the amber honey—transparent but tangible. Delectable.

To crown it all, Batiushka was seeing fewer visitors. He begged the men in black robes to leave him alone, and he hid in the bushes or behind his cabin at the sound of approaching peasants.

"I must now concentrate on the Joy of all Joys if I am to weather this storm," he said.

Joy heard her name and was pleased.

The best moments of all came in the evenings, when Batiushka would kneel before a picture of a lady, which he hung from a branch of an old tree in the clearing. He sang all the songs from the cave, the hilltops, and the garden, one after another. He would sing as the moon rose, until his voice faded away and he knelt, staring not at the picture but almost through it, at something far beyond, which Joy couldn't see. She sometimes went to check behind the picture—he was so filled with rapture he never noticed Joy's sniffing—but there was nothing there. She would lay at his feet until he woke from whatever trance he was in, and then he would give her another bite of bread before she returned to her den for the night.

The storm hit them separately on one such evening. Joy was curled up in her cave like an enormous dog, her nose tucked under one paw, when it descended on her.

There was no noise, no change of smell, but immediately she woke and let out a cry like a frightened cub. Darkness was on top of her.

Have you known such a feeling?

Have you felt it crushing you, a despair so great that you must scream, or strike out, or curl into the smallest ball just to survive it?

Joy had.

It was why she'd come here in the first place.

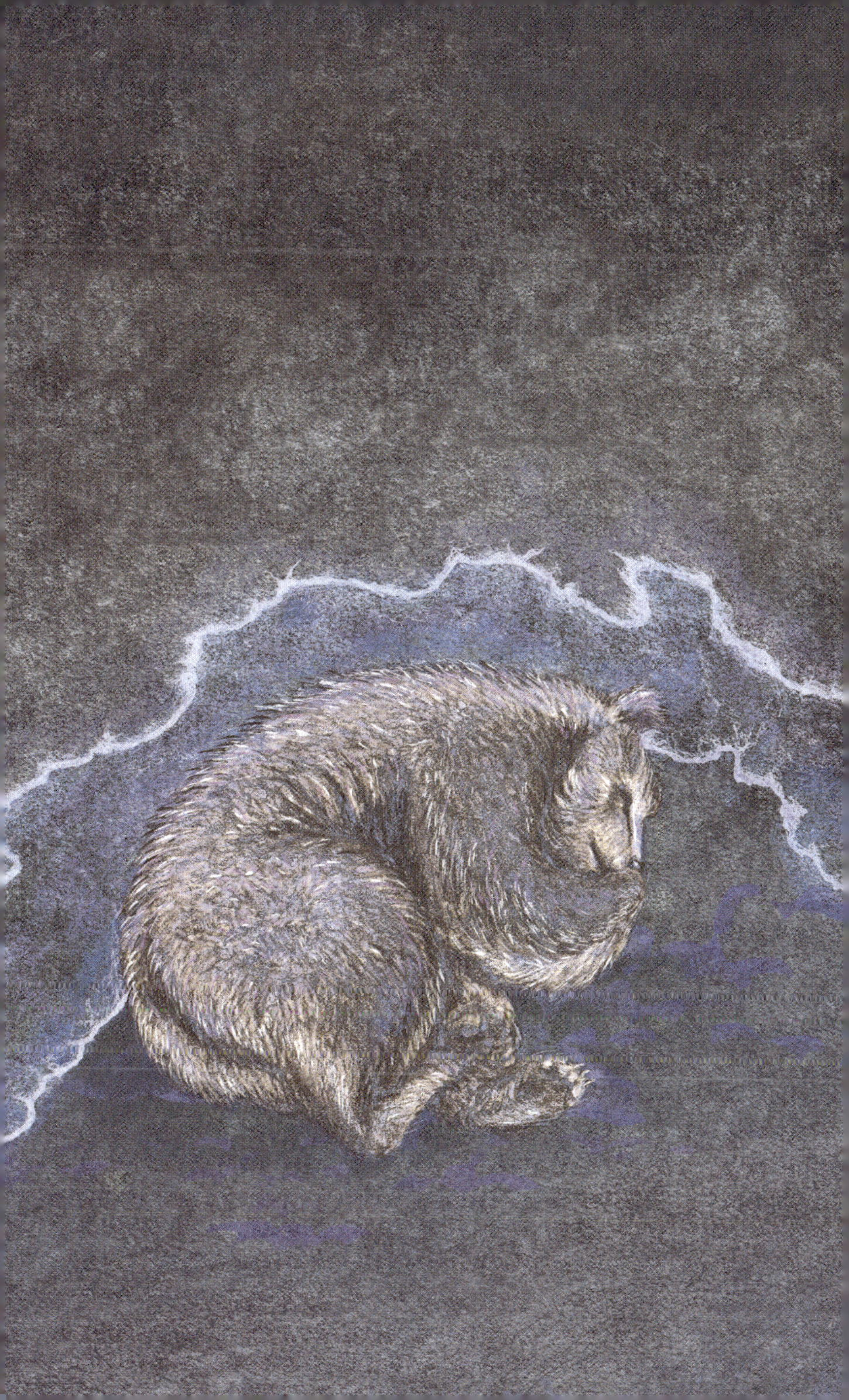

It had felt like emptiness then, but now it was a giant hand closing its fingers around her. It clawed at her empty womb.

She staggered out of her cave and ran for the clearing.

Joy ran as fast as a deer. She ran as though hunters were at her back, as though a pack of wolves were on her heels. No matter how fast she fled, she couldn't outrun the darkness.

The air in the clearing was noticeably colder. It broke over her like a wave as she left the trees. The darkness was thickest of all here, and it enveloped her completely as she raced to the cabin. She scratched at the door and roared for help. She knew only Batiushka could make this go away.

The door opened.

Inside was the dead of winter and the darkest of caves. Batiushka's searching hands felt her nose and poked her in the eye before finding the ruff of her neck and pulling her in. He was muttering a prayer under his breath, over and over, and didn't stop for a moment to say a word to Joy.

She could feel the cold dark heavier on him even than on herself. She felt they were sitting at the bottom of a deep well, so deep that no light or warmth could penetrate. The sun was gone forever, she thought. She lay on the rough pine boards and shivered.

Batiushka's warm hand grabbed her ruff again and pulled her up with impossible strength, pointing her nose to the eastern corner of the hut. He said his prayer louder.

Joy obeyed him and stood, even though her legs shook. When he let go of her fur, she put her nose in his hand just to feel something warm and alive.

It is difficult to tell adequately of the darkness they found themselves in for the long hours of that first night. Perhaps you yourself have felt it at some point in your life and even now shrink away from the memory.

It was the presence of loss. A crushing emptiness. As cold is merely a lack of heat—*more nothing than thing*—and yet so powerful it can kill, so this darkness was an absence of good. An impossible void only held together like a bubble by some boundary of hatred.

And in the middle of this darkness was Batiushka, indiscernible in the black, but *real*—breathing, emanating warmth from his weak little human body, speaking the prayer over and over, words that kept them alive and together.

Joy stood beside him and was a great comfort and very little help in the humble way of an animal.

She did not understand. She was not a human, and she had no prayers. But she was a living creation with a beating heart, something real and not of the darkness. Her nose in the man's hand was a warm, damp reality that kept him tied to the earth.

When the
first rosy streak
of dawn pierced the
cabin window, the darkness
finally dissipated. Normal sounds
of bugs and birdsong returned.

Batiushka coughed and swallowed. His voice had grown hoarse throughout the night. "Glory to Thee, our God, glory to Thee for all things. Glory to Thee, our God, glory to Thee for all things..." he croaked, bowing to the icons—finally visible—and kissing them each gratefully.

Joy collapsed on the floor, shaking the boards and sending pine needles skittering every which way.

The man returned to the bear and gave her some bread from his pocket. "I did not expect they'd be bothering you as well, my Joy."

Joy inhaled the bread and snuffled at his pocket for more.

"You are a comfort to me." He pulled out another piece. No matter how flat his pocket looked, there was always more bread somewhere inside.

Joy thought they would spend the whole day napping in the sun and recovering. She did so, in fact, while Batiushka weeded the garden and picked the vegetables that had ripened. Meanwhile, he took buckets to the creek to fetch water and gathered dry branches for a fire to cook soup. As she lay in a warm patch of grass and felt his shadow pass back and forth over her, she considered an idea that had never occurred to her before.

Maybe a man could be stronger than a bear, small and frail though he was.

She was afraid to return to her den that night, so she slept under the eaves of the cabin. Nothing happened.

CHAPTER THREE · 43

The night passed quietly. Not in deathly silence but a healthy quiet of trees rustling, bugs chirping, and living things breathing peacefully in their dens. Joy stayed wide-eyed and alert for the first hour after darkness, then finally fell asleep listening to Batiushka's voice chanting inside.

> *"He hath made me to dwell in darkness,*
> *as those that have been long dead.*
> *Therefore is my spirit overwhelmed within me;*
> *my heart within me is desolate.*
> *I remember the days of old; I meditate*
> *on all Thy works; I muse on the work*
> *of Thy hands.*
> *I stretch forth my hands unto Thee:*
> *my soul thirsteth after Thee, as a thirsty land.*
> *Hear me speedily, O Lord: my spirit faileth:*
> *hide not Thy face from me,*
> *lest I be like unto them that go down*
> *unto the pit...."*

The morning dawned cheerful and innocent. Joy was glad. Whatever terrible presence had haunted them that night, it had moved on now to other prey, and they might be happy again.

And they were. For three days.

It returned at midday.

They were in the place Batiushka called Gethsemane, the saddest and quietest of places, and he was kneeling with his head on the bench, praying. Joy was sitting behind him and idly watching a bumblebee bob drunkenly about in the grass, wondering if it belonged to a hive she hadn't plundered yet. She'd just decided to follow it home when the darkness slipped over them.

The bumblebee stuttered in its flight and buzzed frantically to stay in the air.

Joy heard its wings beating as though she were inside the cabin and listening through the windowpane. Her own heartbeat sounded twice as loud. She was all alone in the vast darkness with her empty womb like a frozen stone in her belly. She forgot about the bumblebee, about the clearing. She was alone alone alone, just her in the darkness that went on forever.

A familiar voice started the prayer again.

Not alone. Batiushka.

The darkness around them tightened at the sound of his words, and Joy felt the air tremble angrily. It was almost comforting, as malevolent as it was, because it shattered the illusion of nothingness.

CHAPTER THREE · 45

Joy pulled herself up to stand by Batiushka in the darkness of midday. She could feel the hairs rising on her back and a protective fury welling up in her. She planted her front paws on the bench, bared her teeth, and roared at the unseen enemy.

Nothing happened.

She roared again, kicking away the bench, then settled with a low, continuous growl as the darkness ignored her.

Batiushka didn't miss a word in his prayer, but he patted her fondly on the shoulder.

The darkness lasted an hour. When it suddenly evaporated, the sun was still high and bright in the sky, and the man and the bear stood blinking at each other.

Batiushka had been crying.

Joy licked his cheek. It was salty.

He wiped his eyes and went to right the bench.

This time he sat for a few minutes before he returned to his chores, gripping the bronze cross he wore around his neck.

The bear sniffed him to make sure he was not wounded. His weeping always worried her. She had never leaked so much water from her own eyes.

Batiushka caught a drop collecting in a curl of his beard and held it out for her to smell. "Just tears, my Joy. More powerful even than teeth or claws. That's why they left."

She didn't understand, but licked up the tear and lay down at his feet. She was glad he was sensible enough to rest this time.

CHAPTER THREE · 47

The beautiful summer was spoiled. Joy found herself beset by a very un-bearlike anxiety, something like the constant watchfulness of a hare, waiting every moment for the predator to spring out of nowhere. The darkness fell at unexpected times, and Joy learned to steel herself and stay close to the man when the cold emptiness descended.

She had no idea what it was or where it had come from. All she knew was that it came for Batiushka. After that first night, it never bothered her unless she was in his presence. She could feel it coldest around him, and all she could do was stand there and be a warm body to lean against when he grew too tired to stand.

She could have left and gone back to her old forest, but she didn't. In the back of her mind was the faint memory of the days before Batiushka, when she could never forget the tiny darkness in her empty womb. In this great darkness, at least, she was not alone.

Batiushka went about his days as he had before the darkness arrived. He weeded his garden and made soups of beets and cabbage. He chopped the ugliest of potatoes and replanted the pieces, tossing a chunk to Joy every now and then. They climbed the hills together

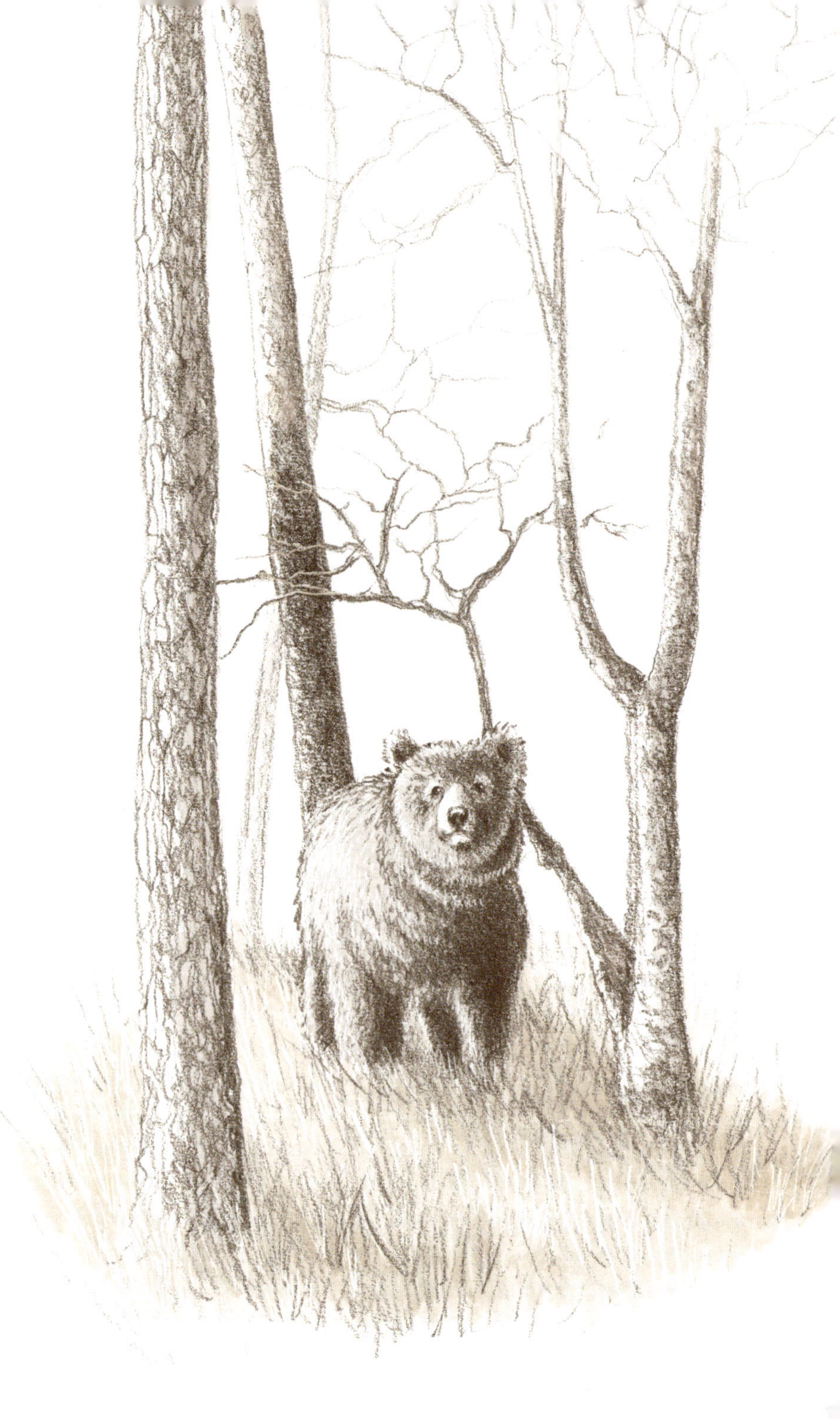

to pray and knelt by the bench in Gethsemane to weep. Whenever the darkness fell, they stopped, and Batiushka chanted his prayer for an hour or so until it went away.

Joy wondered if it followed him on the days he went to visit the men in their buildings outside the wood. She had the sense—she didn't know why—that the deathly silence would not like the loud bells or voices joined in song any more than she did.

All the same, she waited anxiously in the trees each time until he returned.

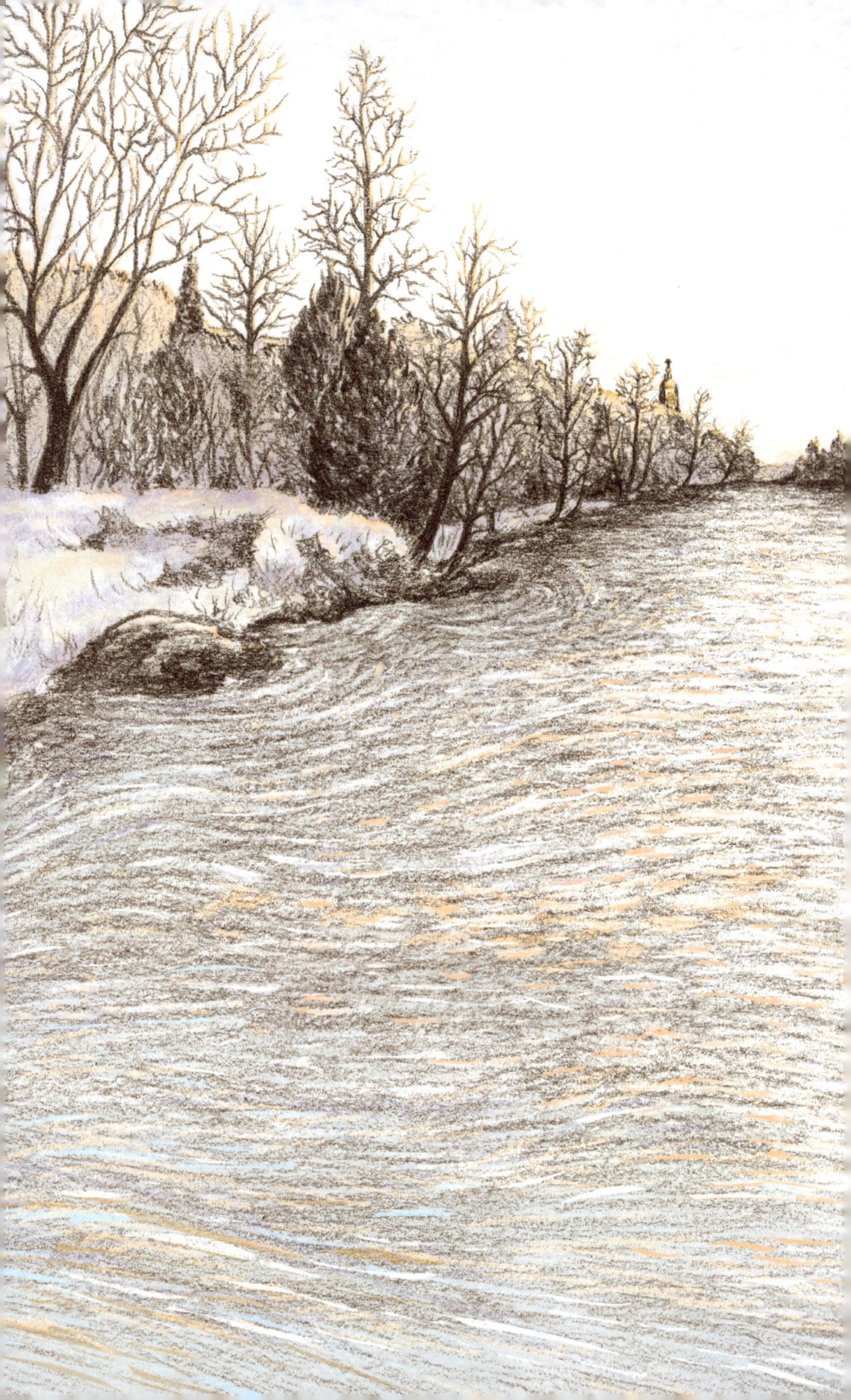

CHAPTER FOUR

Each day was shorter than the last.

Joy felt an urge to wander. Instinct told her to look for farther rivers and better fishing grounds, but she could scarcely go a few miles before worry turned her around again. She was afraid to be separated from Batiushka. She would not hibernate then, just as she had not the previous year.

Batiushka took care of her. He still fed her impossible amounts of bread from his pockets—where did it all come from?—but rarely ate anything himself. He lived on the vegetable soup that was little more than boiled water from the river.

Joy didn't notice.

The chill in the air was cheerful and exciting, so different from the dead cold of the darkness that still found them at odd hours. In the mornings frost glittered on the cabin roof like white diamonds. Each night the stars shone brighter in a cobalt sky.

Joy's fur grew long and thick. Batiushka wore a heavy brown coat and leather mittens that made his hands look much like Joy's paws. He only shed them after a few hours' work in the garden, when the sun cut through the golden leaves and melted the frost.

When the last of the cabbages were picked, washed, and put in jars to pickle, the old man harvested handfuls of the earth itself and spread it on the cabin porch to dry out. He swept the dried earth into old tins and stacked them inside the hut.

Joy never questioned his actions anymore.

When the oak leaves had all fallen and the only color in the wood was the green of fir and spruce, the attacks of the darkness changed. They began to fall regularly, at midday.

At first Joy was relieved to no longer fear the invisible enemy at any moment. Soon, however, she began to dread this new struggle even more. To know with gloomy certainty that each day fear would descend at noon turned the sun's cheerful ascent into the menacing advance of an executioner. The relief after the darkness vanished in the afternoon quickly changed to anxiety. As the sun went down, they felt the whole thing was about to begin again.

Try as she might, the bear could never quite ignore the sun's position in the sky, or how many happy hours they had left before the struggle. And the hours could never be quite as happy when she was constantly aware of them slipping away.

There were times now when Batiushka glanced at the sky and broke off midsong as he trudged to the cave he called Bethlehem. Joy would look at him anxiously as he moved his hand in a cross over his chest, but he'd only shake himself and pick up where he'd left off.

He fought it hard. He gathered pine branches, cones, and candles, and arranged them around the cave. He stayed longer there than ever before, letting the garden disappear under a blanket of leaves as he spent each morning praying. Shortly before noon they made sure to return to the cabin so Batiushka could stand before the icons when the darkness fell.

Joy stood behind him in the cabin one such day,

waiting for the darkness, when she was caught off guard by a gust of wind. Its force pushed her forward a step, and it knocked Batiushka to his knees. The candle in front of the icons went out.

The hour had come upon them, but instead of black stillness, there was wind everywhere. It crashed around the tiny space like a wounded animal, rattling the walls and knocking over the tins of dried dirt with a clatter. Joy hunched her shoulders and dug her claws into the floor to stay on her feet.

Batiushka struggled to get back up again, but the wind threw him into the corner and pinned him down.

Joy heard a sound in it like laughter.

It picked up the man and slammed him back on the floor.

Batiushka cried out in pain. "*Gospodi!*"

More laughter. The wind slid him across the floor and rolled him into the dirt from the tins. It drowned out the sound of his prayers in its roaring.

Joy was too frightened to help. She stood frozen as the wind raised the spilled dirt in a spiral around the man.

It lasted until the bear was so tired that she almost couldn't be afraid anymore. Then suddenly the wind

CHAPTER FOUR • 55

died, sending a last puff of dirt into her face for good measure. She snarled, pawing at her face to clear her eyes. When she could see again, the cabin was quiet, and Batiushka huddled on the ground, shaking.

Joy was at his side in a moment. She licked his face, but he would not get up or look at her.

"Why would He not help me?" he said, tears in his voice.

Joy was ashamed. She had not protected him when he needed her most. She licked his face again, and when he ignored her, she went and sat outside on the porch, her ears flattened against the back of her head.

It was nearly sundown when Batiushka finally came out. He sat down next to her and stroked her head gently.

She couldn't meet his eyes.

"I have asked to grow stronger, so I should not complain when I'm given heavier burdens," he said, finding a crust of bread for her in his pocket.

She took the bread meekly but would not look up at him in case he was angry.

"We mustn't despair," Batiushka said quietly. He drew her enormous head onto his lap and scratched the soft corner between her ear and jaw. Brown hairs fell on his white robe and danced away in the breeze. "The trials are permitted to strengthen us, not destroy us. God is merciful."

Joy understood none of this. She only knew he had cried out for help when the wind took him, and she had done nothing.

He bent over and looked directly into her huge, brown eyes. "This is my struggle alone. Do you understand me?"

She chuffed and blinked at him.

"No, a master mustn't teach an apprentice a skill that he himself doesn't understand," he said. "But you are permitted to me, my Joy, because you are a small, simple thing."

She sensed affection in his voice and closed her eyes, letting out a long sigh.

They sat like that until it was nearly dark, and Batiushka left Joy on the porch to go back inside and clean up.

She watched the trees and listened as he swept the dirt back into the tins and relit the candles, singing something quietly under his breath.

"Have mercy on us, O God,
have mercy on us—
for in Thee have we put our trust—
do not be angry with us,
or remember our iniquities,
but look down on us even now,
since Thou art compassionate,
and deliver us from our enemies,
for Thou art our God and we are Thy people.
We are all the work of Thy hand,
and we call on Thy name."

As she walked back to her den that night, she heard the bells ringing in the buildings far off, and smelled something nearby. She had reached the crags of rock where the caves began, not far from Bethlehem and her little hollow. She stood on a stony outcropping and sniffed for wolves or hunters. A soft footstep would make no sound here.

It was a good scent, a combination of the salty aroma of human, sweet milk, and some flower Joy knew could not be blooming this late in the year. She sniffed deeply and looked upwind in the direction of Bethlehem. A light flickered in the caves.

Had Batiushka gone out to pray so late? She could do with another bite of bread before sleep.

When she reached the mouth of the cave, she saw the light had only been the moon reflecting on the gold leaf of the picture of the mother and baby in the wooden box. She sniffed it—it did smell like milk, and she even gave it a lick to make sure it wasn't good to eat—but it was only wood and paint.

Because she was only a bear, Joy left it at that. There was no Batiushka here. There was no bread. She returned to her den and slept deeply until late the next morning.

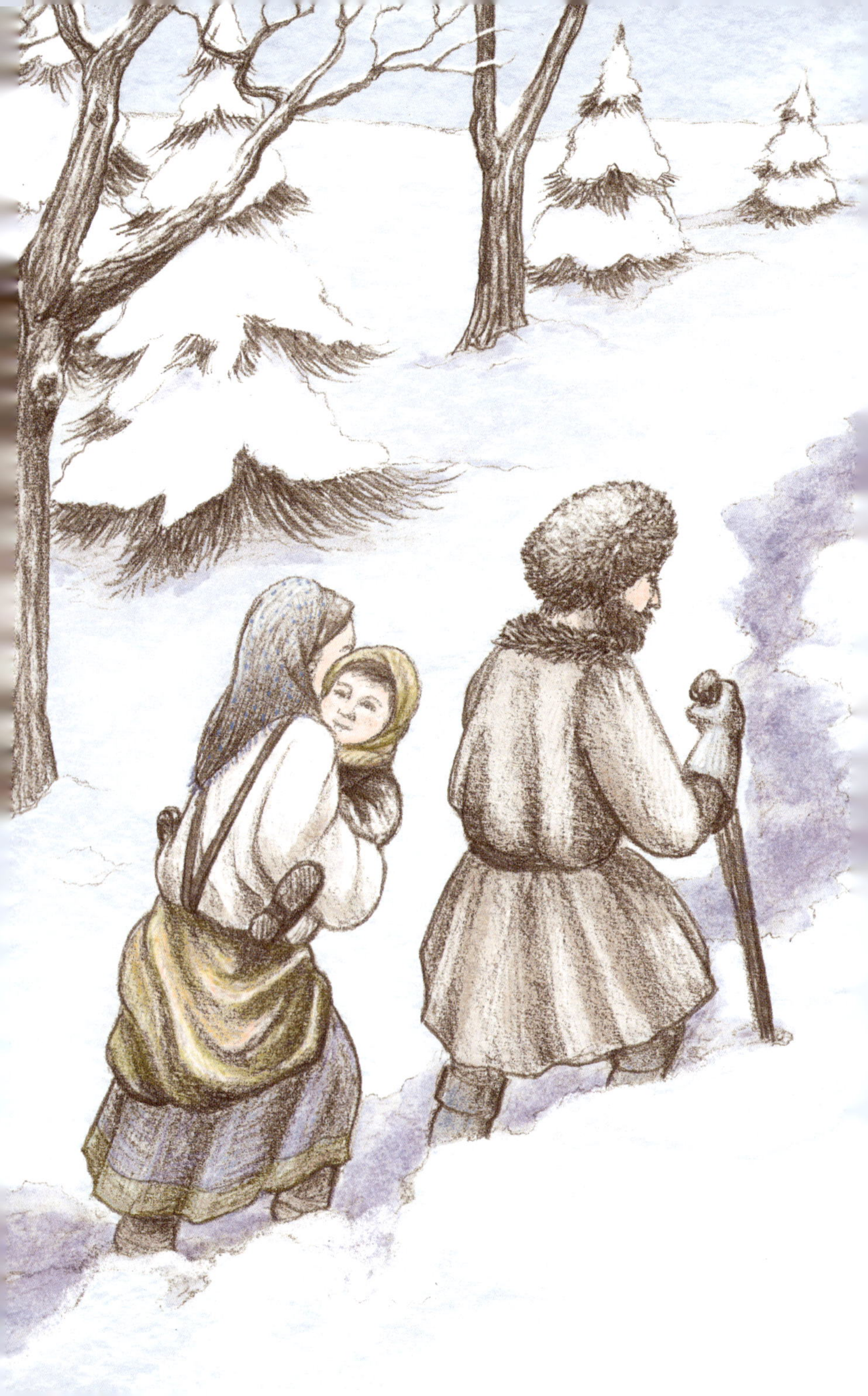

CHAPTER FIVE

Snow lay in a heavy, sparkling coat over all the wood. Pilgrims crunched through it, bundled in furs and laughing merrily as they journeyed to see the staretz, the Batiushka who was growing famous for his advice. He hid from visitors, it was said, but if you brought children with you, he could not resist when they called and pled for him to come out. He was rumored to have a strange knowledge of everyone's personal affairs. He could read a man's heart like the little Gospel he kept in his cabin.

Joy was unhappy with the rise in guests, and hid sulkily in the Bethlehem cave, where Batiushka would join her when he had spoken to the pilgrims and sent them away. The more talkative they were, the wearier he became, and the attacks of the wind seemed worse on the days after visitors had left.

"I can't turn them away, but I'm not strong enough to fight this battle and carry them along as well," he said to Joy on one such afternoon. He was lying on his back in a snowbank, where the wind had lifted him high into the sky and dropped him. It was gone now, but he was too tired to rise.

Joy chuffed. If he didn't want to send the humans away, she would be happy to do it for him.

"I must think. I must pray and ask the abbot what to do."

The bear turned an ear southward as they heard children calling in the distance. "Batiushka Seraphim? Where are you? Please, please come out!"

Batiushka closed his eyes. "I should go help them. Poor things."

Joy rolled over to lie down on his feet.

One night Batiushka washed in the icy river and walked down the path to the monastery, even though he had just returned a day ago.

Joy followed him to the edge of the trees as she always did, anxiety at the change in routine rising off her like

CHAPTER FIVE · 63

steam. She laid back her ears and widened her eyes pitifully when Batiushka kissed her forehead as a goodbye, but he was not dissuaded. In fact, the pat he gave her on the shoulder was a little brusque.

If she had been a woman, she might have read into it a bit more. But she was only a bear.

He was gone until the next evening, and when he returned he was in good spirits, smelling of sweet smoke, unfamiliar spices, and all sorts of delicious things.

Joy nosed at him and found to her great satisfaction that some of the smell came from the pastries hiding in his pocket.

"*Kristos rozhdaetsya*, my Joy," said Batiushka, fishing out a bun sweetened with honey and dividing it three ways between Joy, a marten, and a fox who had also come to wait for him.

Because it was evidently a special day, Joy ate her share of the bun without bullying the marten and fox into giving her their portions as well.

Batiushka led them through the woods and back to his cabin, scattering the remaining crumbs from his pocket onto the snow for the birds. When they turned a corner, he came up short.

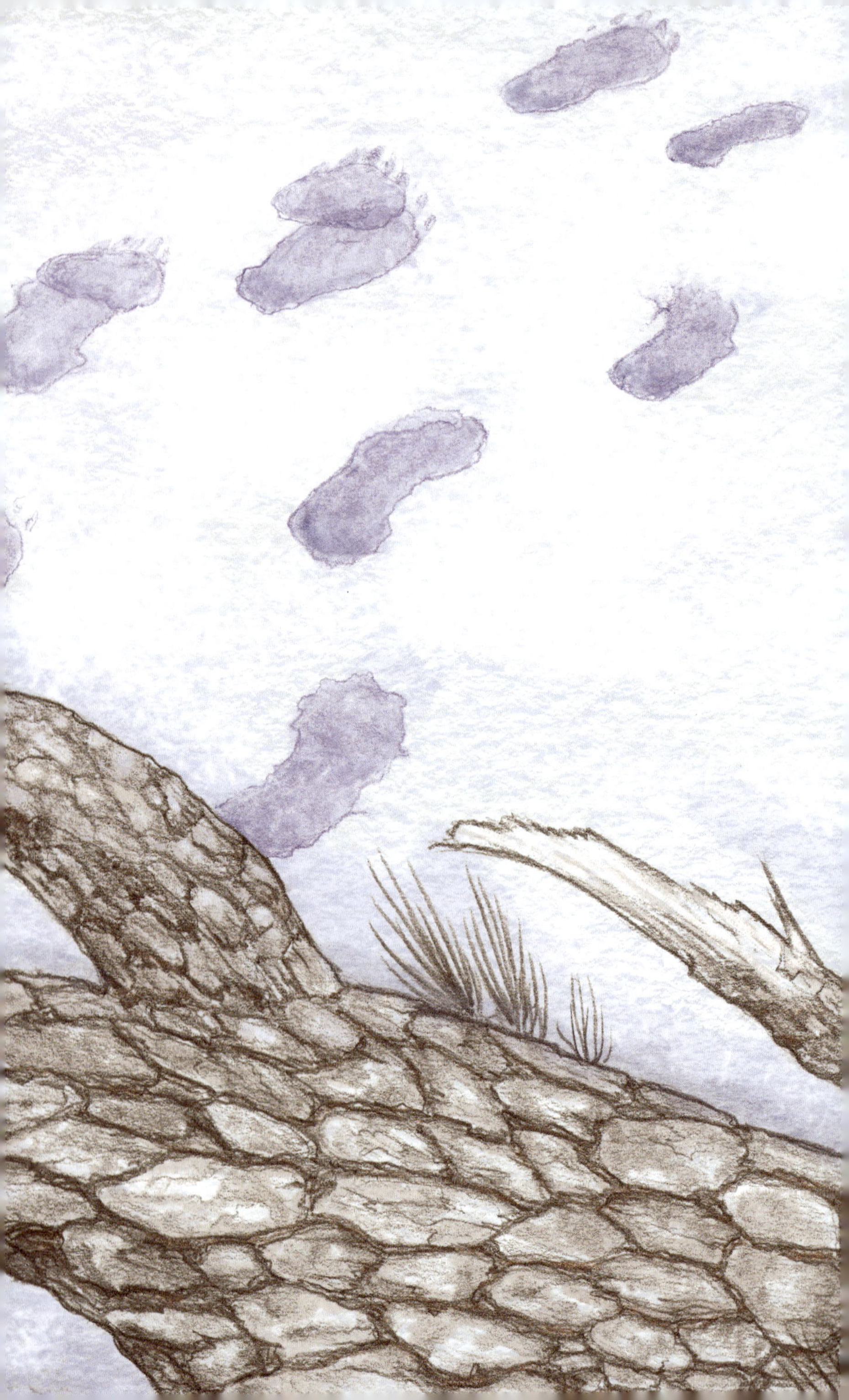

A tree had fallen across the path during the night. He put out a hand and touched the rough bark as a smile spread across his face.

"What an answer, my Joy!" he said. "I have been praying about our visitors, whether to let them come or turn them away for now. I could not have asked for a clearer sign!"

Joy, the fox, and the marten watched as he pulled more fallen branches across the road, piling them high around the tree. The fox twitched his bushy tail uncertainly, thinking this was perhaps a game.

"I don't wish to be unkind," he explained to the animals, casting off his coat and wiping his brow as he warmed up.

The marten sidled over to make sure the coat pockets were indeed empty. Joy rumbled at him softly, though she'd wondered the same thing.

"But this is the answer for now," Batiushka went on.

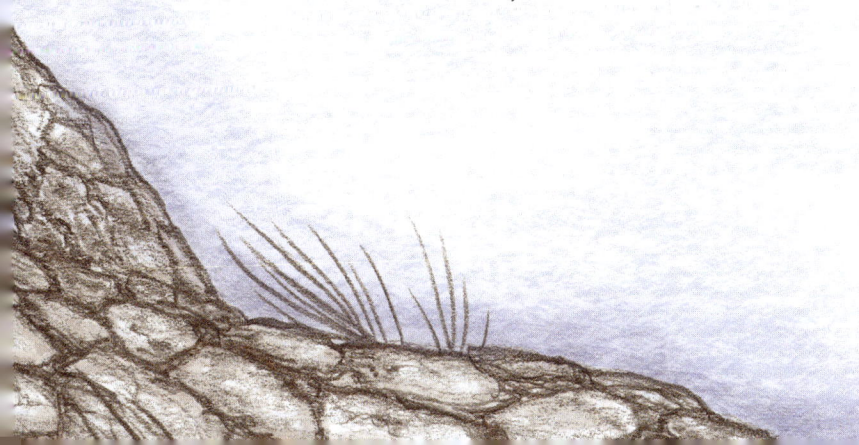

"No more visitors for the time being. Until these trials pass and I can be of real use to them."

They went to the Bethlehem cave and spent several candlelit hours in prayer and singing. Two hares showed up, and the moose, and numerous squirrels and birds, until the cave was so crowded that the air was warm with the heat of bodies. No one could move without stepping on a paw or a tail. Joy was so busy wishing everyone else would leave, she didn't wonder at all when Batiushka gave them gingerbread cookies from the pockets that had been empty earlier.

Neither the fox nor Joy considered eating any of the smaller creatures, nor did the hares and squirrels fear them. That was how it was when they were with Batiushka. In his presence, they instinctively adopted the old way of beasts, as if some ancient memory of a garden and a name-giver lived inside them.

When Batiushka finished his prayers, he kissed the icon, laid it in the manger, and left the cave. The animals flooded out after him, returning to their dens and nests.

Joy watched them leave with a tinge of scorn. She alone followed him back to the cabin. She was rewarded with a scratch behind the ears and one last scrap of gingerbread.

CHAPTER FIVE · 67

"Why do you follow me so, my Joy?" asked the man. "Monks, laymen, and beasts have come to see me, and none have stayed like you have."

The bear sniffed in a disparaging manner. Obviously because she loved him the most.

Batiushka looked strangely sad. He petted her snout with a callused hand. "I would send you away and spare you some of it like I do the others."

One morning in spring, Joy woke early and walked through the woods to the clearing. The birds still slept in the trees above, and the only sound was the crackle of twigs under her paws and the rumble of her empty stomach. She hoped Batiushka's pocket would produce some more treats. Something that needn't be shared with others.

Batiushka was already outside and sitting on the boulder when she arrived, stroking the ears of an enormous brown bear.

She came to an abrupt halt at the edge of the trees and stared, dumbfounded.

She hadn't seen another bear since she had come to these woods. It was a male, rich brown in color, and much, much larger than her. As she watched, the wind blew Joy's scent toward the couple, and she saw the bear's nostrils flare.

He turned toward her and rose on his hind legs curiously.

Batiushka waved.

Joy stayed exactly where she was. She could see bread crumbs on the male bear's muzzle, and it made her feel something inside, something like the dark emptiness that preceded the evil wind.

Batiushka called to her. "My Joy! Come and meet your brother!"

She came forward slowly and gave the new bear a cursory sniff. He smelled of deer flesh, and there was some dried blood still clinging to the fur at the corner of his mouth.

She was only a bear, but if she had been human, she would have sneered. She had forgotten by now, of course, that she herself used to eat other animals. Only until recently she had craved fish.

Batiushka seemed not to notice at all how disgusting the other bear was. He clapped them both joyfully on the back. "Look at this reunion!" he said, beaming. "He-bear and she-bear, at peace with each other, man, and beast for the first time since your forebears left the ark! I went into the desert and found a new Eden."

He took two pieces of bread from his pockets and fed them to the bears.

Joy watched glumly as the male bear ate his share. She was sure he'd gotten the larger piece.

Batiushka called the newcomer Misha.

The male bear took a cave near Joy's for his den—much to her annoyance—and followed Batiushka around like a large, stupid dog. He took loads of branches on his back like a donkey when they built a fence around the garden to keep out the rabbits, who, in spite of their love for the old man, could not resist the temptation of cabbage. He helped the old man dig rocks from the ground with his claws. He stood shamefacedly when Batiushka berated him for taking a nip at one of the squirrels who hung around the cabin.

"Everything you need will be provided, if you only trust," said Batiushka, pulling more bread from his pocket and stroking the traumatized squirrel.

Joy sat a distance away and glowered at them. *She* was not offered bread, and she had behaved herself. It was terribly unfair.

Of course, she did not go ask for any, or she might have been given some.

The only times Misha did not hang around were during the fits of wind that still came at midday. During these times he ran and hid in his den like a cub.

This had the very strange result—which Joy either did not notice or did not admit to herself—of her looking forward to those attacks just the tiniest bit. They were now the only times she was alone with Batiushka, when she was his faithful support when all others failed.

The worse the wind battered the old man, the more Joy felt he was lucky to have at least one bear as loyal and devoted as she was.

She did not notice that the wind grew wilder and more fiendish as her thoughts took this direction, or that Batiushka took longer to stand every day when the hour had passed. The more he trembled when she helped him up, the more pleasure she felt in being his only support.

This pleasure soon became the only one she had, as Misha was always around to ruin the rest of them with his presence.

Batiushka himself seemed to be pulling away from her. He had not said as much, but now the glances he gave her were weary and sad. He looked happier, if it were even possible, to be with a clumsy beast like Misha, who was always making stupid mistakes, than with Joy, who was incomparably wiser and more sophisticated, almost Batiushka's own equal.

One day Misha had not shown up, and Joy was feeling simultaneously scornful and pleased with his absence. She and Batiushka were in the garden with the bench, where he had often wept beside her. Batiushka was praying, but his voice was exhausted, and he stumbled over

CHAPTER FIVE · 73

his words. Suddenly he turned to Joy and stared at her.

It was so unlike him that she quickly scrambled to all fours—she had been lying in the sunlight—and flattened her ears guiltily without quite knowing why.

"What am I to do with you, my Joy?" he said sadly.

She sniffed hopefully at his pocket.

"You should thank God you are not nearly as sophisticated as you think," he said, pulling out a crust and feeding it to her from his palm. "Else you'd be in much greater trouble."

She wasn't really listening, just enjoying the bread.

"Go home," he said.

She looked up, startled. She knew what the command meant.

"Go home." His voice was stern. "You are doing more harm than good today. Come back when you are soft again."

Surely not? Surely she had misunderstood? But he was pointing sternly back toward the caves. Joy took a few steps and looked back.

He was facing the bench again and praying.

The day was still bright and sunny, but everything seemed dark. Joy slunk back to her cave and huddled in the corner, listening to Misha snore next door.

Near dinnertime the snoring stopped, and the offender made sniffing and smacking sounds as he woke up. After another moment he poked his head around the opening to Joy's cave, an idiotically friendly expression on his face, as though to say "Hullo, neighbor!"

Joy turned around purposefully so that her tail was facing him, and flattened her ears to show her displeasure.

He sniffed around for a little bit then trundled off, probably to be with Batiushka.

CHAPTER FIVE · 75

She stayed in the cave all night. She might have stayed in the morning, too, except that she was feeling a bit humbler on an empty stomach.

At the mouth of her den, she stopped. Misha had left a slightly smushed piece of bread on the ground for her.

Joy blinked at it.

It is ridiculous, of course, that darkness could be overcome by a morsel of bread.

But then again, Joy liked bread very much.

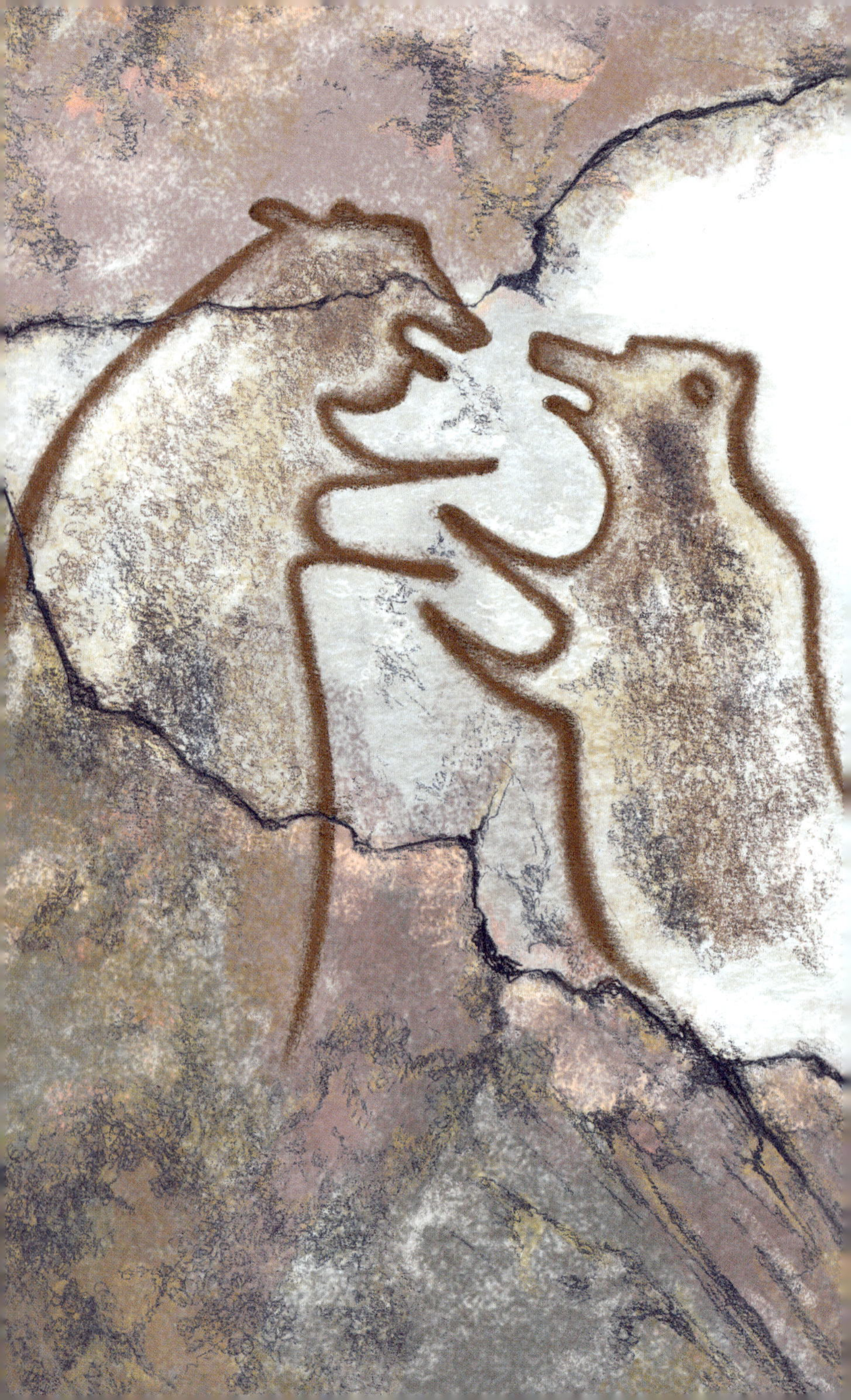

CHAPTER SIX

When the first man and first woman were cast from the garden in the earliest days, there was a fracture among the animals. The strongest and wisest among them saw that flesh tasted better than grass, and they preyed upon the weaker ones, turning in some cases upon their own brethren and even their own offspring.

The he-bear became violent and greedy, and the she-bear grew to fear and resent her mate. When he took one of his own cubs for food, the she-bear became his enemy.

The bears have no language for stories, being only dumb beasts, but in the mysterious way of animals, they retain the ancient knowledge of this fracture. It is known, as the spider knows to spin a web and the goose knows to fly south in winter, that there is no love between bears, except between mother and cub.

But all that changed when Batiushka Seraphim made his little cabin in the woods of Sarov.

Joy lay in the cabin, her head buried in Batiushka's lap, thinking of all these things as the evil winds howled.

Today the winds did not enter the little room with the icons and the cheery, crackling fire, but contented themselves with buffeting the walls, rattling the glass panes in the windows, and pushing the door against the latch. Sometimes the winds sounded like wolves, other times like children crying out. Joy heard the mewling of a cub again and again. She couldn't help but shake.

Batiushka petted her head and said his prayers louder to drown it out. "...Son of God, have mercy on me, a sinner."

The wind beat on the door like fists. The phantom cub cried.

"*Gospodi, pomiluy. Gospodi, pomiluy.*"

When the hour had passed and the wind had vanished, the man eased from prayer into song. He added oil to the lamp in front of the icon of the mother and child—the "Joy of all Joys," as he called it, much to the bear's confusion—and prostrated himself many times before kissing the image.

"*Radusya devo...*"

Joy waited humbly until he was finished.

He returned and finished his song with his hand on her shoulder. They stood quietly together for a moment.

"I am glad you are back," said Batiushka. "You are a comfort to me."

He spoke no more words about her sulkiness for the past months. When Misha came a few minutes later, looking for bread, the two bears lay peacefully beside each other at the old man's feet.

How shall we write of the love of beasts?

How can a bear love her master with all her heart and yet come to love one of her own kind in fullness as well?

Did they come to love one another more because of the love of the man who bound them together?

Love grew slowly, with gifts of bread, loads of firewood carried together, and naps taken back to back in the sun.

Misha was warmth and ease, uncomplicated. He had no gnawing hole inside him, just simplicity and satisfaction. If he was not as clever as Joy, she found in time that it made him better company.

He never managed to stay with them for the hour of fear.

"Do not trouble yourself about it," Batiushka said to Joy one day as she looked sadly into the trees where Misha had wandered off. "We should not give him a burden too heavy for him to bear." The old man rose slowly from the porch to go inside. "There is great strength in knowing one's limitations."

The forest turned green again with new leaves, then orange and red, then white with snow. The bull moose ceased to visit, and no one knew whether he had moved on, or had died. Joy soon forgot all about him, as creatures do. She and Misha shared a cave together, and the months and years turned in a great circle marked by the snows and distant church bells. At the center of the circle was always Batiushka, moving from Bethlehem to Gethsemane and back again.

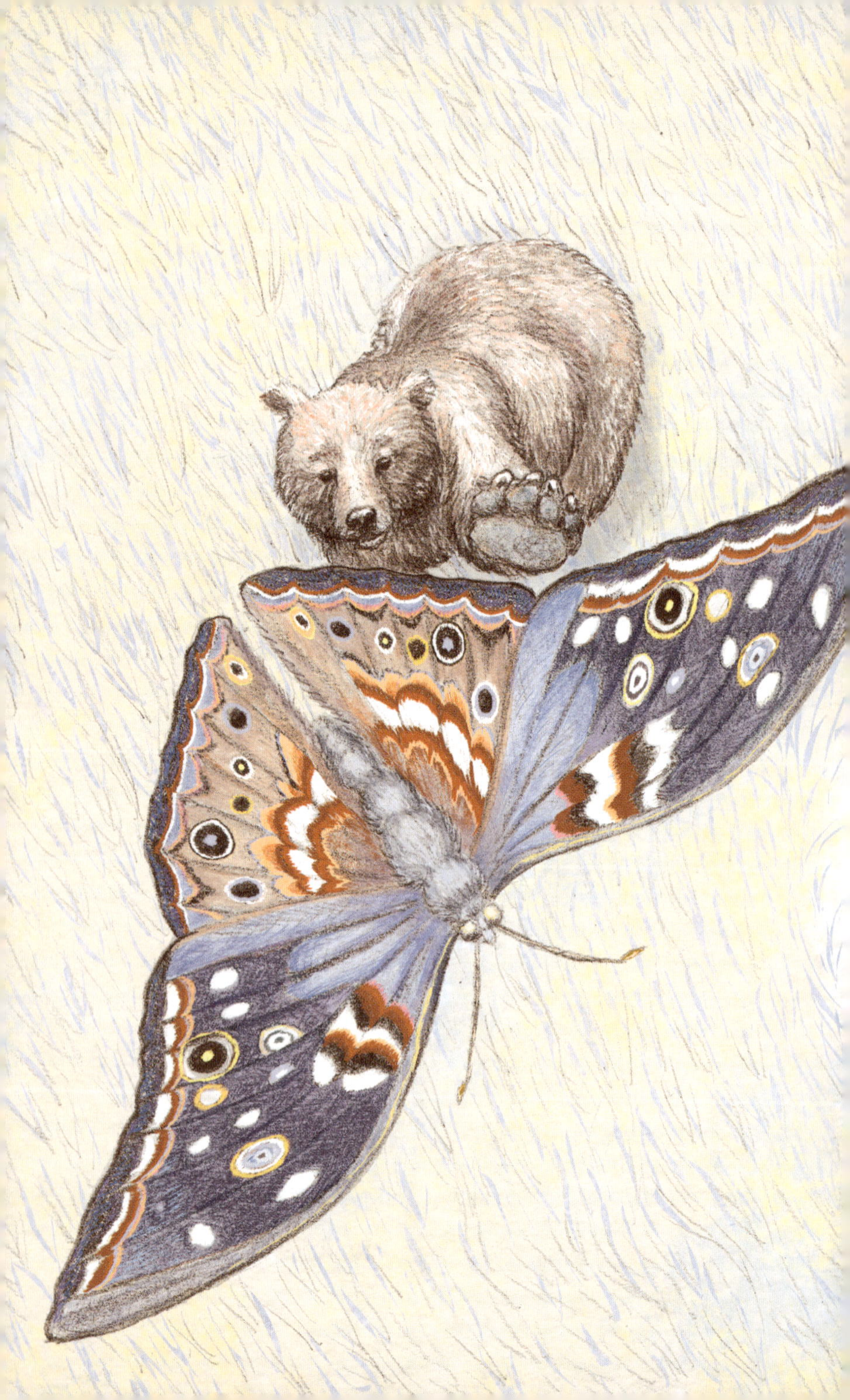

CHAPTER SEVEN

Misha was unlike Joy. He was like the birds and rabbits, filled with a love as simple and warm as sunlight. He came happily from his cave whenever he happened to rise, did whatever Batiushka asked of him, and went back when the old man grew still in prayer or went indoors. What Joy had taken for stupidity and laziness was something more like contentment and peace.

There was no cub between them, but there was warmth.

The warmth was more welcome now than ever, because something had come over Batiushka, something that troubled Joy greatly.

It was like the cold darkness in its despair, and like the howling winds in its intensity, but instead of hanging in the air around them, it had taken up residence upon Batiushka himself. It lay coiled over his shoulders and around his neck like an invisible snake, weighing him down with a dreadful heaviness that sometimes caused him to stagger. It was worst before prayers, and at night, so that Joy hated leaving the man alone after dark when she returned with Misha to their cave.

Batiushka bore the weight silently. He barely said a word anymore, even to the bears. Only in prayer did he speak, and it seemed a great effort.

Misha seemed not to notice anything different in the old man, but Joy saw something in Batiushka's eyes that frightened her—a weariness of life itself. She wondered if the trials were too much. She grew quiet and sad herself in his presence, and it was only Misha who kept them from sinking down altogether.

"Acquire a spirit of peace, and all around you will feel peaceful," Batiushka said late one summer afternoon, cracking a rare smile at the sight of the male bear chasing a butterfly around the clearing.

Misha let the butterfly escape and dropped to the ground to scratch his back against the boulder. He rose again with bits of moss stuck to his fur, panting slightly, and gave Joy a friendly lick on the cheek.

CHAPTER SEVEN · 87

She touched noses with him in response and lay her chin on Batiushka's lap again.

"My Joy, your worry over my burden is becoming a weight of its own," Batiushka said, looking down at her.

She couldn't help it.

Then there came a week when Batiushka did not go to the buildings of men at the edge of the trees.

Nor did he go the next week.

Or the next.

There was no more bread, not even in the all-producing pocket, and he ate only handfuls of the dry, sunbaked dirt kept in sacks in the cabin.

Joy was alarmed.

"The passions are destroyed by suffering and afflictions," was all he said.

He went no longer to the cave of Bethlehem or the top of the hill to pray, neither to the garden bench, but hung his most precious icon from a tree in the clearing. When the sun set, he hobbled to the boulder and knelt upon it with his arms upraised to pray in front of the icon.

Misha had already gone back to the cave and was sleeping peacefully, Joy was certain, but she remained. She lay by the boulder in case Batiushka should fall; his arms trembled from fatigue and lack of food.

> "*Gospodi Iisuse Khriste, Syne Bozhiy,
> pomiluy mya greshnago.*"
> "*Gospodi Iisuse Khriste, Syne Bozhiy,
> pomiluy mya greshnago.*"
> "*Gospodi Iisuse Khriste, Syne Bozhiy,
> pomiluy mya greshnago.*"
> "*Gospodi Iisuse Khriste, Syne Bozhiy,
> pomiluy mya greshnago.*"
> "*Gospodi Iisuse Khriste, Syne Bozhiy,
> pomiluy mya greshnago.*"
> "*Gospodi Iisuse Khriste, Syne Bozhiy,
> pomiluy mya greshnago.*"

On and on went the prayer, deep into the night.

Joy drifted off and woke in darkness, and Batiushka's prayer still went on.

"*Gospodi Iisuse Khriste, Syne Bozhiy, pomiluy mya greshnago.*"

Until the words were like the years, revolving in a never-ending circle, encompassing Joy until she forgot they were there at all.

And still Batiushka knelt with his arms outstretched.

When the sun rose, Joy awoke again. Batiushka's voice dropped to a whisper and was silent. He sagged from the boulder and onto Joy's broad flank.

She rolled over carefully, easing him to the ground.

He lay in the grass, eyes closed. Was he all right?

She sniffed him. Something was different.

"The despair was gone," he whispered hoarsely. "For eight hours, there was joy." He smiled.

She caught her name and the smile and was pleased.

"Run and fetch me victuals, my Joy," he said, still not opening his eyes.

She obeyed, dragging a sack of the dried dirt to him. Perhaps he had gone mad, but somehow she smelled life in him that had not been there for a long time.

During the day he weeded the little garden, tended the bees that he kept in a hive by the cabin, and read his books. The invisible weight hung on his shoulders again. From time to time he would slump over as he drifted off with weariness, then straighten with a little jump, shaking himself and turning back to his task.

Joy kept a close eye on Batiushka.

CHAPTER SEVEN · 93

Misha kept a close eye on the bees.

There was no bread for supper again. Joy ate grass, and Misha wandered off to find something better. He did not look back, either in displeasure or in appeal, which was his way.

The sun set. Batiushka set down his book and walked slowly to the boulder. He hoisted himself up, and knelt, raising his arms with upturned palms.

Joy swallowed the last bite of grass, and went to stand by him.

> *"Gospodi Iisuse Khriste, Syne Bozhiy,*
> *pomiluy mya greshnago."*
> *"Gospodi Iisuse Khriste, Syne Bozhiy,*
> *pomiluy mya greshnago."*
> *"Gospodi Iisuse Khriste, Syne Bozhiy,*
> *pomiluy mya greshnago."*

The air grew cooler. She felt a little pang in her heart when she thought of Misha's warm body in their cave, and her empty spot beside him.

> *"Gospodi Iisuse Khriste, Syne Bozhiy,*
> *pomiluy mya greshnago."*
> *"Gospodi Iisuse Khriste, Syne Bozhiy,*
> *pomiluy mya greshnago."*

> *"Gospodi Iisuse Khriste, Syne Bozhiy,
> pomiluy mya greshnago."*

Batiushka's voice trembled, and he shifted back and forth on his knees. The boulder was rough, and the ridges of the stone hurt him. He stood for a while.

> *"Gospodi Iisuse Khriste, Syne Bozhiy,
> pomiluy mya greshnago."*
> *"Gospodi Iisuse Khriste, Syne Bozhiy,
> pomiluy mya greshnago."*
> *"Gospodi Iisuse Khriste, Syne Bozhiy,
> pomiluy mya greshnago."*

His legs shook. They were swollen and weakened by an old illness. He knelt for a while.

> *"Gospodi Iisuse Khriste, Syne Bozhiy,
> pomiluy mya greshnago."*
> *"Gospodi Iisuse Khriste, Syne Bozhiy,
> pomiluy mya greshnago."*
> *"Gospodi Iisuse Khriste, Syne Bozhiy,
> pomiluy mya greshnago."*

Joy felt again that all time disappeared. They were in an eternal moment of darkness, with Batiushka's prayer revolving in circles around them, just them and the weariness and the pain of his legs and the pain of the hole inside her, magnified by Misha's absence.

> "Gospodi Iisuse Khriste, Syne Bozhiy,
> pomiluy mya greshnago."
> "Gospodi Iisuse Khriste, Syne Bozhiy,
> pomiluy mya greshnago."
> "Gospodi Iisuse Khriste, Syne Bozhiy,
> pomiluy mya greshnago."

The struggle was eternal. There would be no end.

> "Gospodi Iisuse Khriste, Syne Bozhiy,
> pomiluy mya greshnago."
> "Gospodi Iisuse Khriste, Syne Bozhiy,
> pomiluy mya greshnago."

CHAPTER SEVEN · 97

> *"Gospodi Iisuse Khriste, Syne Bozhiy,
> pomiluy mya greshnago."*

A tear slipped from Batiushka's eye, and then another. He prayed and cried. The tears were like the pain falling away. They became tears of relief. Of thankfulness.

> *"Gospodi Iisuse Khriste, Syne Bozhiy,
> pomiluy mya greshnago."*
> *"Gospodi Iisuse Khriste, Syne Bozhiy,
> pomiluy mya greshnago."*
> *"Gospodi Iisuse Khriste, Syne Bozhiy,
> pomiluy mya greshnago."*

Of joy.

Was it madness?

Joy stood until she could not stand, then lay with her head raised until she couldn't bear to hold it up any longer, then dropped her chin to the root of the tree and slept fast through sunrise, when the dew collected on her back.

Batiushka finished his prayer and lurched down from the boulder, lying in the wet grass.

Misha found them there later, sniffed them both curiously, and meandered on, looking for something to eat.

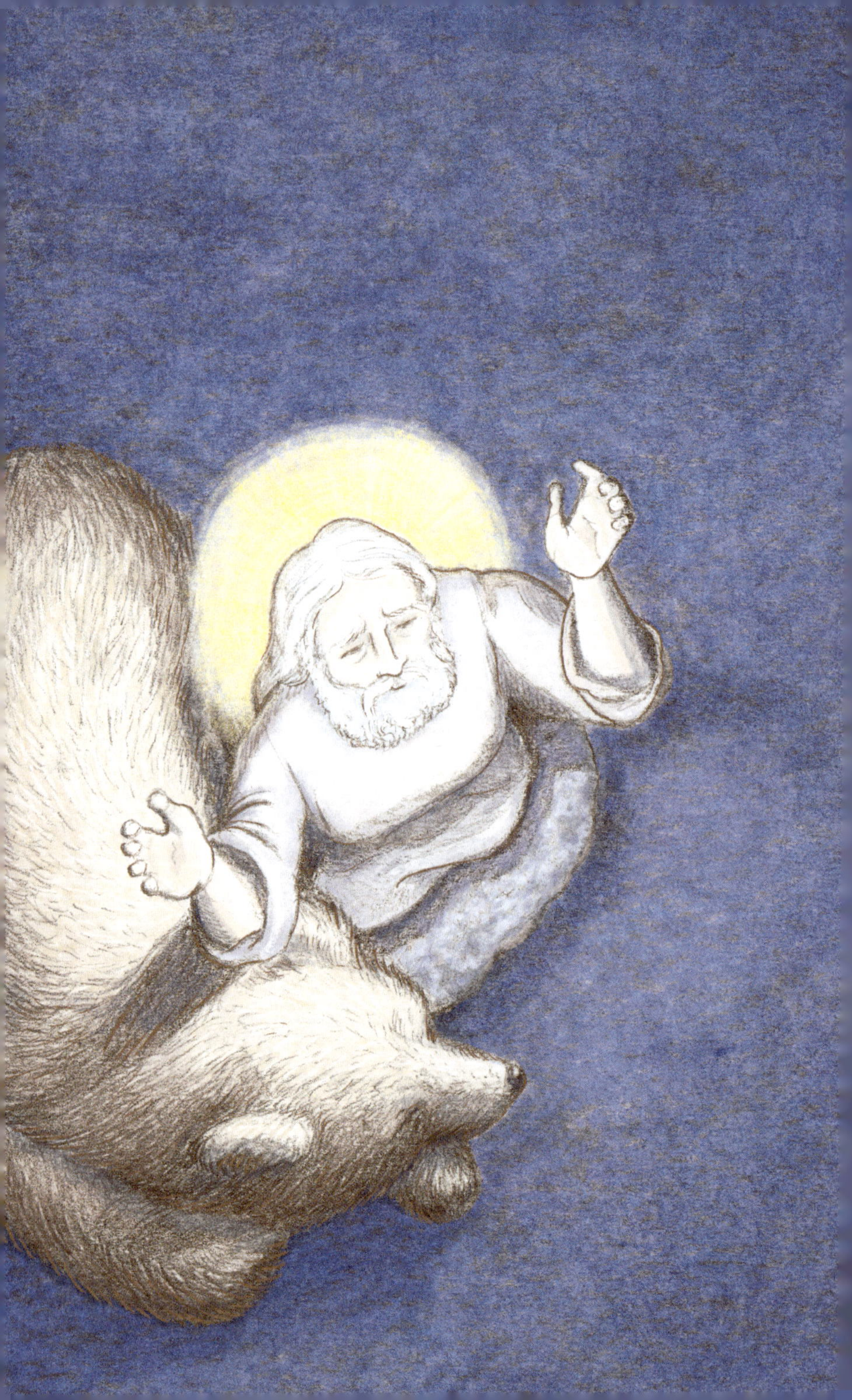

CHAPTER EIGHT

What had seemed a hardship at the beginning became a balm.

The noonday demon hung heavily on the old man and his bear, but each night it fled when Batiushka lifted his hands.

After an hour beneath the stars, with arms upraised, Batiushka's pain vanished and his eyes grew unfocused, as though he saw nothing.

Or, Joy thought, as though he saw something far off that she could not. When this happened, she felt the tension leave him and a great peace radiate out of him, something like the peace of Misha, but magnified a hundredfold. The peace would fill her too, and often she would fall into a deep sleep beside him, comforted as a cub cradled by its mother.

One such night she was wakened by the moonlight shining in her eyes. She blinked at the radiating orb of blue-white, then realized it wasn't the moon at all, but Batiushka's face, so bright that she could barely discern his features.

After that, she was too unnerved to fall asleep anymore during prayers.

Each morning they lay on the grass in exhaustion. The grass became crackling brown leaves, then snow. And on and on and on, flowers and leaves and snow and stars until Joy felt they were an ageless part of the earth, like the boulder itself.

The prayer never ended.

On a snowy day in the second winter, Misha wandered off in search of something better than dirt to eat, and he did not return.

Joy followed his scent until it was buried in fresh snow, and then stood looking into the trees after him for a long time. The emptiness inside her, which had almost vanished in the constant work of prayer and chores, swelled suddenly until she was overcome and lay down in an icy drift.

Batiushka found her there some hours later.

"My Joy," was all he said, and put his hand on her head. They watched the snow fall together until a mantle of white crystals covered their shoulders.

When it grew dark they walked back to the clearing. Batiushka climbed on top of the boulder, sighed deeply, and faced the icon hanging from the tree.

Joy stood by his side, because it was what she did. She felt anger and pain, and didn't understand it. She was only a bear.

"You mustn't judge him," said Batiushka quietly.

Misha had never stayed to pray.

"We who are most sick must seek greater treatment," Batiushka said.

She was silent, as always.

> *"Gospodi Iisuse Khriste, Syne Bozhiy,*
> *pomiluy mya greshnago."*
> *"Gospodi Iisuse Khriste, Syne Bozhiy,*
> *pomiluy mya greshnago."*
> *"Gospodi Iisuse Khriste, Syne Bozhiy,*
> *pomiluy mya greshnago."*

The image of the woman on Batiushka's icon caught the icy blue of the snow in the moonlight. Her eyes downcast, her hands folded over her chest in acceptance, she seemed to come in greater and greater focus in Joy's eyes until the snowy wood around them shrunk, rippling, into the icon.

> "Gospodi Iisuse Khriste, Syne Bozhiy,
> pomiluy mya greshnago."
> "Gospodi Iisuse Khriste, Syne Bozhiy,
> pomiluy mya greshnago."
> "Gospodi Iisuse Khriste, Syne Bozhiy,
> pomiluy mya greshnago."

And on and on and on, into the night, into the icon.

No other bear carried such an emptiness inside, and no other bear was permitted to witness this mystery. She did not ponder these things or treasure them in her heart, for she was only a bear. But she stood beside her master and listened to the words she did not understand, and her spirit said,

Let it be.

The seasons turned around the rock and the old man and the icon. A thousand nights, and the demon draped around him like a stole at last departed, at least for the time being, to go bother someone else. It could not live on a body fed by dirt and prayer.

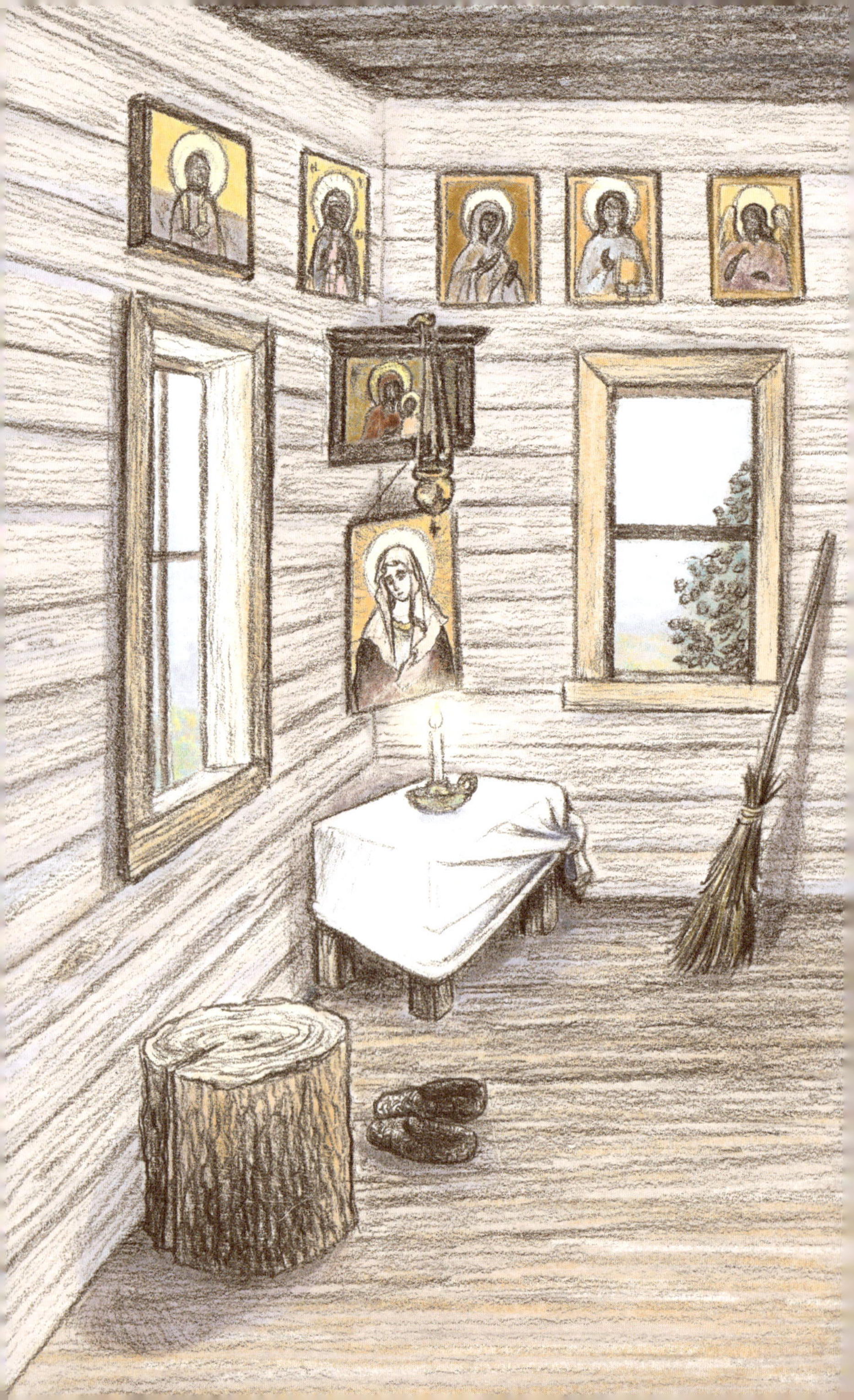

CHAPTER NINE

At the dawn of the thousandth day, Batiushka lowered his arms and grew quiet. He did not fall to the ground as usual, but slowly climbed down from the rock and hobbled to the tree. He kissed the Joy of all Joys icon and went back into the little cabin.

Joy followed him, her joints creaking. She was feeling very worn down these days. If she crossed her eyes slightly, she could see streaks of silver on her muzzle.

Batiushka kissed the icons on the wall in the corner. Then he sat down wearily on his bed of stones, and motioned for Joy to sit next to him.

She did so, taking up most of the free space in the room.

"My mind says it still," he murmured to her.

She rolled her eye up to him at the sound of his voice, but was too tired to do anything else.

"I am always praying now, even when I am silent. Is it the same with you?"

Joy closed her eyes again and hoped they could go to sleep.

"This is a great mercy given to me," he said to himself.

Joy snored a little bit, just to get the point across.

Batiushka reached his hand into his pocket, and miracle of miracles, pulled out two pieces of bread, both of which he gave to Joy.

She forgot about sleep momentarily and gulped down the morsel. It was the first bread they'd had in such a long time. It must have been in his pocket all along, but it tasted as fresh as though it had been baked that morning.

"What a victory," said Batiushka. "I dread whatever they will throw at us next. God help us. They have been despicable, and lately, without any subtlety at all. It frightens me to think…"

Joy's sniffing and nosing for more food interrupted him.

"But you are right. After the fast must come the feast, and after sadness, joy, or we have missed the whole point." He smiled at her and pulled more bread from his pocket.

They walked together to the caves, past the one Joy had shared with Misha, past the cave of the Nativity, which still smelled faintly of some strange spice, and to a little hollowed-out space in the hill, where lay some old linen cloths.

Joy hoped they would take a nap together in the little cave, but instead Batiushka raised his head to the sky and called out in a loud voice,

"KHRISTOS VOSKRESE!"

The rocks echoed back an answer.

"KHRISTOS VOSKRESE!"

Birds wheeled down from the sky and came to land around him. Hooves and paws thudded in the forest around them as every beast came to the sound of his voice.

"KHRISTOS VOSKRESE!"

Batiushka's face grew bright, as though an inner light shone through his thin, wrinkled skin. The light filled

the cave and shone
on the animals' faces
until they could only see
the dazzling brightness. A great
warmth was everywhere, as though they
were in the flame of a candle, and yet they felt no
pain, only an incredible joy. The bear thought the joy
was Batiushka.

"*Khristos voskrese iz mertvikh, smertiyu smert poprav
i suschim vo grobekh zhivot darovav!*" Batiushka cried.

This was victory. Joy could sense it. This was the light

that chased away all
darkness forever. This was
the joy that filled all emptiness,
the end to every sorrow. Beyond this
light was nothing, she was certain, because in
the light was everything good in all nature, brought to
fulfillment. She felt these things as only a bear can.

    They ate of the bread from Batiushka's pocket, every animal, until they were satisfied, and Batiushka as well, then rested together in the sweet green grass. When the sun set beneath the caves, Joy was already fast asleep.

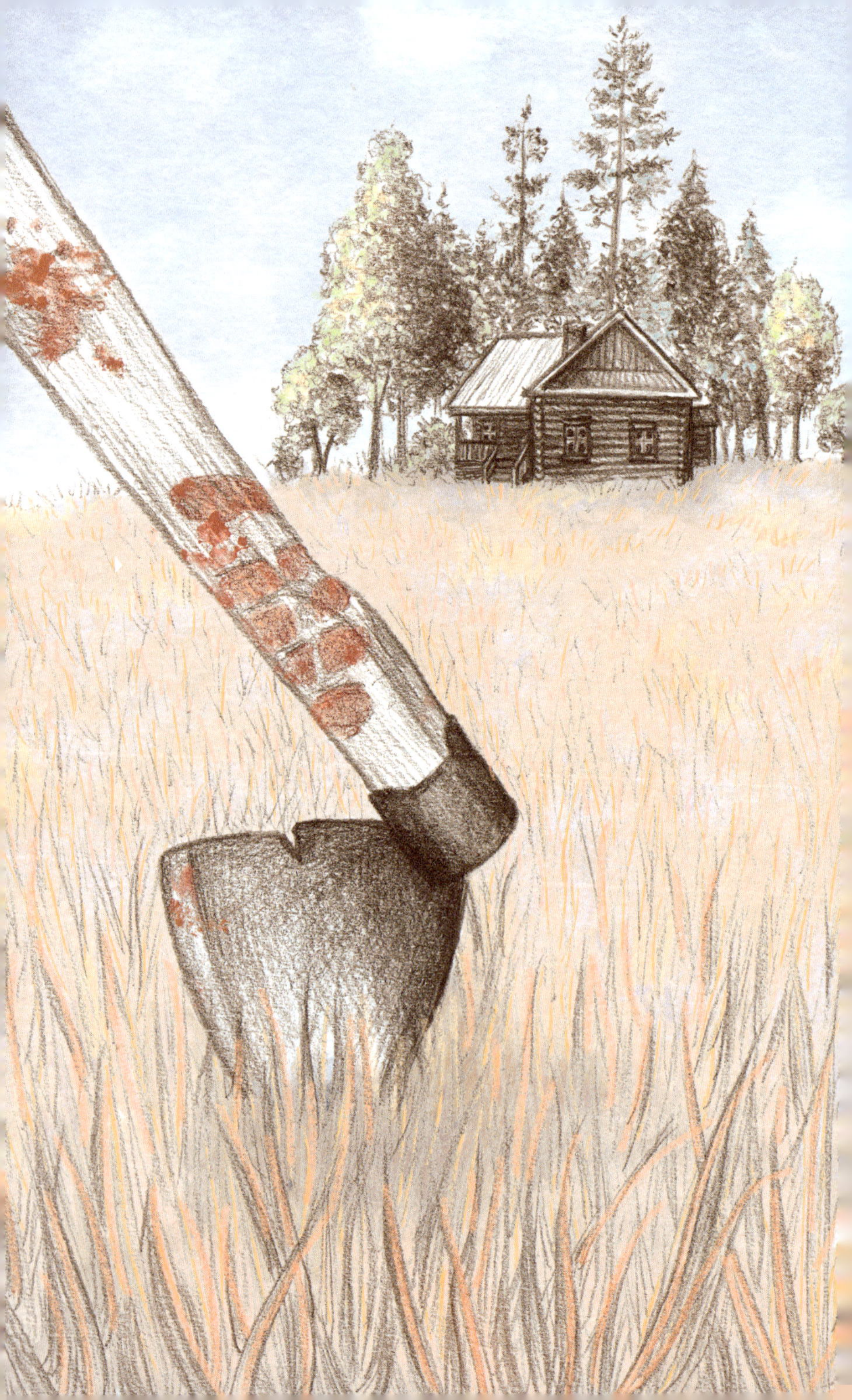

CHAPTER TEN

Had she not overslept, well past dawn and into the warmth of midmorning, it might never have happened, because she would have been there. Maybe it was a wicked imp that shrouded her eyes and kept her dreaming. Or maybe an angel, that the old man might face his great trial unhindered by any earthly care.

Or maybe she overslept because she was getting old herself and was only a bear.

For whatever reason, she slept, and Batiushka met the three men alone.

When the warm sun slipped over the crest of a rock and into Joy's eyes, she awoke expecting to see Batiushka's face shining in front of her.

The other animals had long since vanished, and the cave was empty.

A feeling of unease pricked her, as often happens when one wakes in an unfamiliar place. She clambered to her feet, shook the dew from her coat, and trotted in the direction of the cabin.

The woods were cheery, full of birdsong and the rustle of branches on a windy morning. The only thing out of the ordinary was the scent of men Joy came across as she passed the old trail blocked by the fallen tree. No one had visited them from the monastery or the village in so long, she had almost forgotten what other men smelled like. At least three men had come this way, the odor of their sweat mixed with horse and straw and alcohol. Joy felt a surge of anxiety and hurried on as quickly as she could on her stiff paws.

At the clearing she came across some of the tree limbs she and Batiushka had dragged into a heap, half of them chopped up neatly and piled together, with Batiushka's little axe lying a few feet away. The scent of the men was strong here, and mingled with blood. Footprints crushed the grass, and the ground was torn up in places. Red drops peppered the earth. Joy took one look and called out wordlessly. She stood still, listening, and heard nothing.

CHAPTER TEN · 113

The cabin was silent, and the windows dark.

She broke into a run.

The door was shut. She sniffed the red stain on the handle and stood up, pressing her front paws against it until the latch snapped and it swung inward. Joy dropped to all fours as the sun streamed in and across Batiushka's boots.

Something rushed up inside her as she saw him still and bloody on the ground.

Like the rush of tears to the eye or milk to the breast. A sudden collecting and swelling, overflowing, outpouring, weeping. It filled the dark hole where there was no cub, every empty space, swirled to the top of her, and burst out in a cry that rattled the cabin walls.

He lay on his stomach with his head turned sideways, face obscured by the graying hair stuck in the blood on his cheek.

Joy was over him in an instant. She sniffed his face—he was still breathing; she could feel the slight warmth of each exhale—and began to lick away the blood.

One eye fluttered open and squinted at the long tongue cleaning carefully around it, pupil dilating and contracting in an effort to make sense of the image.

The old man's fingers twitched at his side.

Joy kept working.

In a few minutes, Batiushka's face was all but clean, and she had found the wound in his hair, the source of the blood. It seemed to be drying already, and she left it alone, searching for any other serious problems. When she got around to the eye again she saw that it had shut peacefully. She licked the dried blood from around a cut on his swollen lip, then sniffed at his arms, back, and legs.

More was wrong with him than the wound on his head, but other than scrapes on his knees and many dirt and grass stains, she found no outward signs of injury. She licked his face again in hopes of waking him. Nothing. Finally, she lay down beside him, just as they had lain so many times by the boulder after a night's vigil.

His fingers twitched again, tickled by the fur of her shoulders.

She looked over, and his eye was open.

If she had been a human, she might have asked him what had happened.

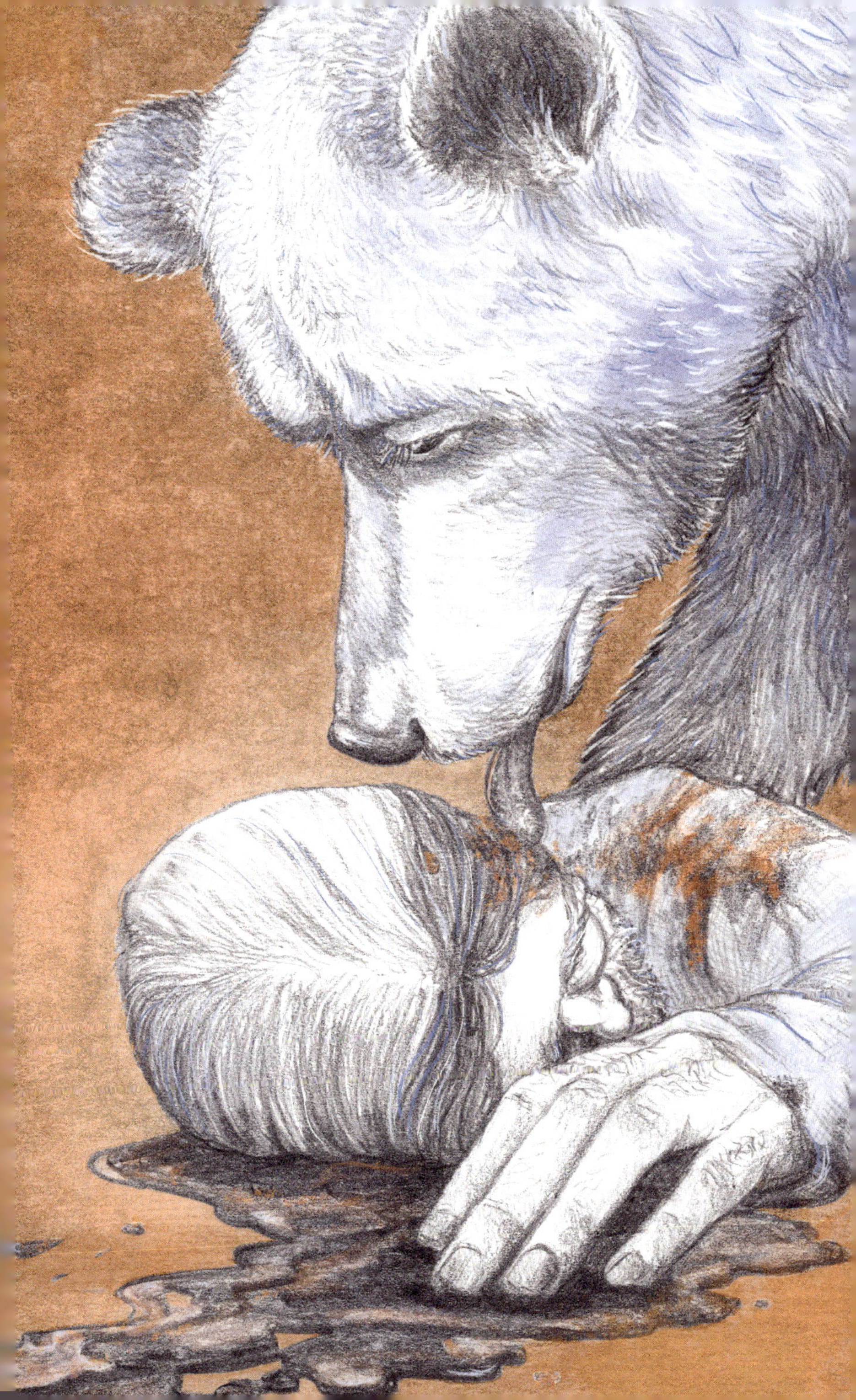

But she was only a bear. She gave his fingers a cursory lick and rested her chin on her paws, waiting patiently for something to change.

The eye closed, and the fingers curled shut in the bear's fur. It was some time before they opened again.

Joy's head shot up. She sniffed the old man's face.

"Christ is risen, my Joy." He choked on the words and coughed, then hissed in pain and clenched his jaw. "But... I'm afraid I cannot."

Joy dug her snout under his armpit to try and help him, but he cried out, and she jerked back, frightened.

"Be still, be still," he said, clutching his ribs, "and I will come to you."

Slowly, *so incredibly slowly*, Batiushka pulled himself up to his hands and knees. He put out an arm, and Joy slid her shoulder underneath it. A few agonizing minutes later, the old man was standing, slumped halfway over the bear.

"You must help me"—Batiushka paused to catch his breath—"to the monastery. They can... help me."

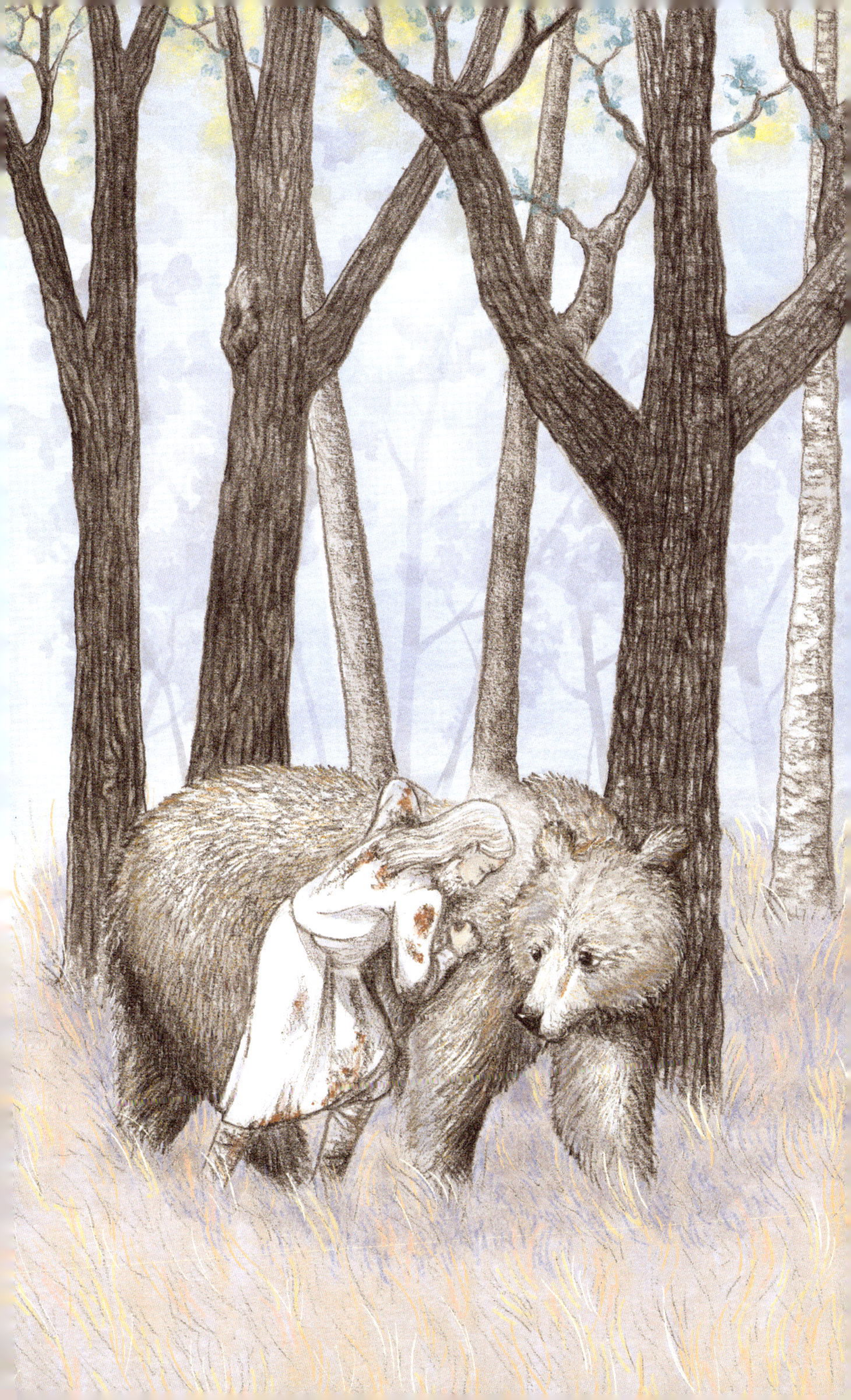

She didn't fully understand, but felt him inch toward the door, and she shuffled along.

"Wait, wait," he said. "We must say a proper... goodbye." With a weak tug on her fur, he directed her back to the corner, where he kissed his fingertips and touched each of the icons in turn. "They sought treasure, poor things, but they didn't even know it when they saw it," he said to himself, lingering over an icon of the woman and her baby.

Joy stood very patiently until he had finished, then they began the slow trip to the door again. She felt him wince with every step, and she tried her best to support his weight.

The sun was high and hot. A few mosquitos found them and took advantage of their slow progress as they made their way through the clearing and into the wood. Joy had thought no creature would ever harm Batiushka, but now someone had nearly killed him, and these infernal bugs swarmed around him to take advantage of his weakness. The world which had seemed so beautiful and sacred the night before had betrayed them.

The path was overgrown from disuse, and they struggled through young saplings and thorns. When they came to the place where the fallen tree lay, Batiushka could not climb over, and there was not space enough for bear and man to squeeze between the log and a neighboring spruce. Every moment they spent staring at the tiny gap, Joy felt the old man's trembling increase, and she grew more and more afraid of what would happen if they could not pass.

Batiushka let go of the bear and sank to his knees. "You must go for help, my Joy," he said faintly.

Joy would have none of it. A desperate fury at the log took hold of her. With a roar that sent birds fluttering from the nearby trees, she rose on her hind legs and pushed against the log. It rocked slightly, but it was cradled deep in the forest loam.

She snarled, pushing it, ramming it with her shoulder, throwing her full body weight against it.

"My Joy, please," Batiushka said, "it's all right...."

She braced her back against the spruce and wedged all four paws against the log, straining with all her might. For a moment nothing happened. Her claws sank into the decaying bark.

Then, with a rustle of dead leaves and snapping of branches, the log rolled up over the lip of its indentation in the forest floor and settled with a thud a meter away.

The gap created just enough space for them to squeeze through.

Breathing hard, Joy went back to the old man and snaked her huge head under one arm. She helped him to his feet, and they shuffled slowly onward as though nothing had happened.

He was silent, struggling to inhale and exhale, but his fingers squeezed twice against the bear's shoulder, and she understood him perfectly.

Step by step they moved toward the far-off dome and cross rising above the trees. It seemed to Joy that it would never get any closer. Batiushka's eyes were closed, and he limped blindly where she led him.

What seemed like hours later, the path joined another that was clearer and well trodden. The smell of men made the hackles on Joy's back rise, but she forced herself to press forward. At least the old man stumbled less on the smooth ground.

Finally, the path spilled out like the mouth of a river into a sea of green, sweet-smelling grass. The buildings of the monastery loomed before them in the brittle, unnatural lines of man-made things.

Joy halted, uncertain. She had never gone farther.

CHAPTER TEN · 121

Batiushka opened his eyes. He took another step forward.

Joy chuffed anxiously.

He let go of her fur and took another step.

She raised a paw and put it down, whining low in her throat.

"It's all right, my Joy," he said, stopping to look back. "You have helped me far enough."

She let out the wordless call again.

All the way from the cabin, she had not realized he would be leaving her here.

Doors slammed, and men in dark robes appeared around the buildings. One of them pointed in their direction, and Joy's ears lay flat against her skull at the shouts of alarm.

Batiushka limped toward them slowly. The sun shone on the few remaining white spots of the robe stained with grass, dirt, and blood.

The men shouted again. They ran toward him.

Joy backed into the shelter of the trees.

She watched to see them lift Batiushka into their arms and carry him off to the buildings. She caught a

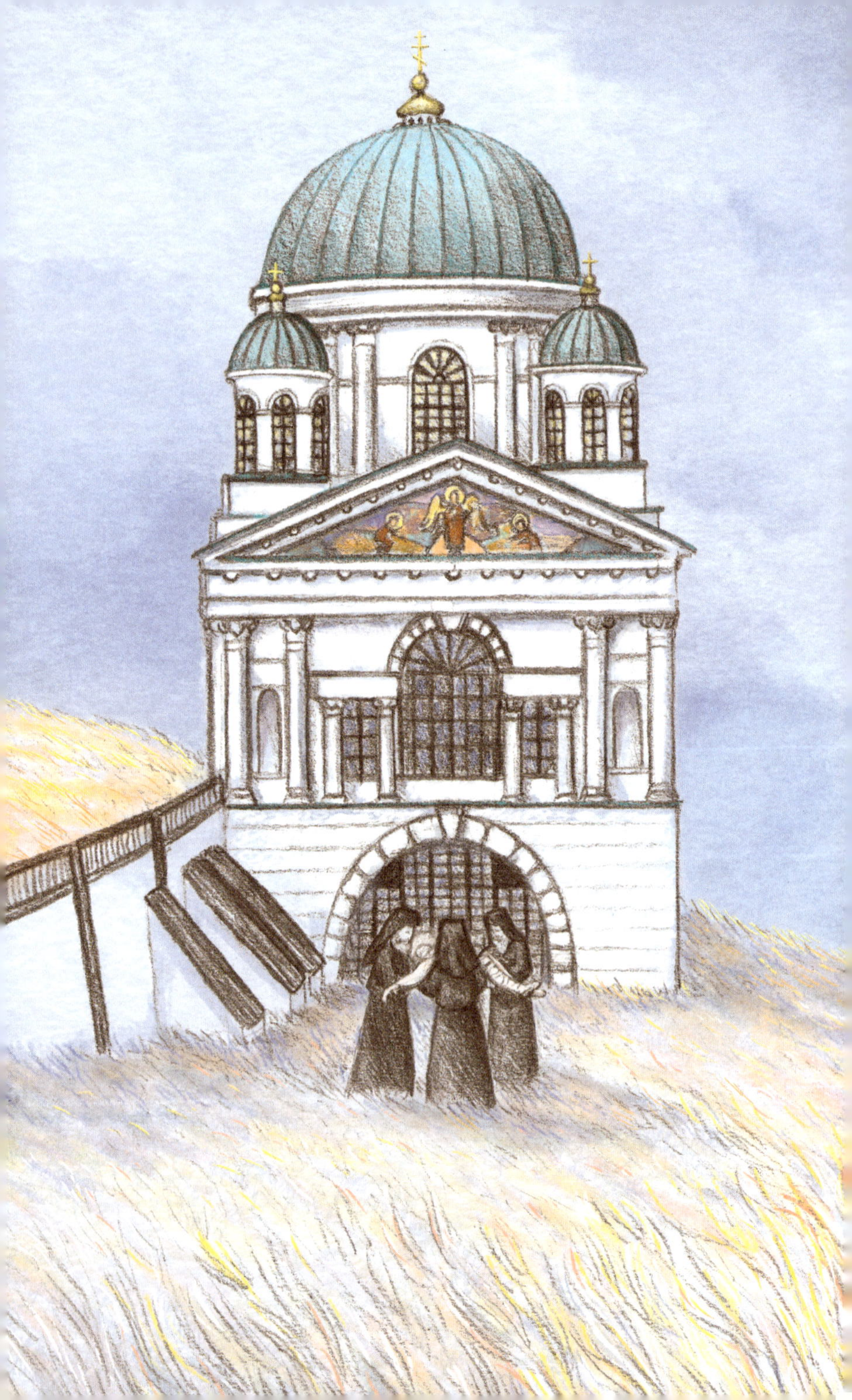

CHAPTER TEN • 123

glimpse of a Lady walking out to meet them, robed in blue, with stars on her brow and shoulders, and a crowd of bright attendants at her heels. The men carried Batiushka past her without looking up, but the old hermit turned his head toward her and murmured something.

The Lady looked to the woods.

Joy felt her gaze and fled to the caves.

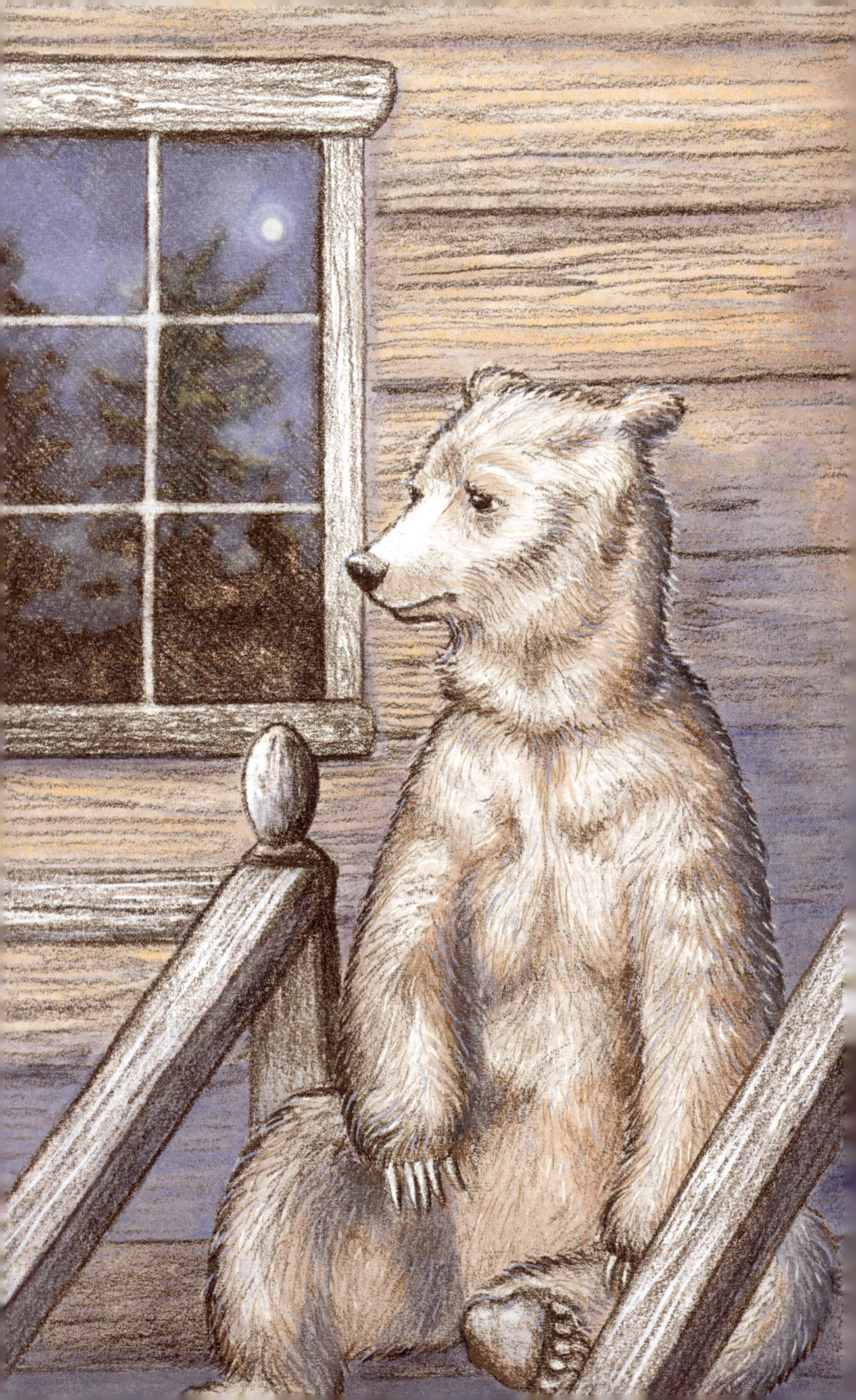

CHAPTER ELEVEN

She lay in the little hollow of rock where Misha used to sleep, which still smelled faintly of him, then went and lay in the Bethlehem cave, and finally went back to the cabin. She sat on the front porch in the odd, slumping manner of bears, and waited.

The sun sank behind the treetops, and the insects sang their evening songs.

She waited.

The moon rose and shone on the clearing, gleaming on the surface of the vigil rock and the blade of the fallen axe. In time the insects grew sleepy and stopped singing. Stars twinkled in the sky as if nothing extraordinary had happened—as if it were any other night, with Batiushka chanting the circle of prayer in front of his icon.

Joy could see it still swinging gently from the tree limb in the breeze. He must have forgotten to take it down in the fervor of the celebration at the empty cave.

If she had been a human, she might have grown angry, thinking of the icon looking on passively from above as Batiushka was beaten and the cabin ransacked. But she was a bear, and only sat wishing she had not been dozing in the sun when it had happened. If she had been with the old man when he was attacked, she would have ripped the intruders limb from limb and laid them at his feet.

She lingered on this last thought in a wistful manner for several minutes and finally let it go with a deep sigh of regret.

He would not return tonight. She would look for him in the morning, or at midday, just as in those years when he still went to the monastery each week. Perhaps he would bring her bread in his pocket, as he had then.

Cheered by the idea, she eased herself down into a ball on the porch and closed her eyes. It would not be long. Surely it wouldn't. The men at the monastery would fix him—men had magical knowledge—and

CHAPTER ELEVEN · 127

then he would return to her and everything would be as it was before. She would sleep on the porch from now on to keep him safe. She need only be patient until he returned.

A day passed.

And another.

Joy ate a little grass when she got hungry, and sat on the porch.

On the third day, she could sense something rising hot and painful inside her. She paced back and forth in the clearing. The Lady in the icon bobbed in the gentle breeze, and Joy had the urge to swat at her. She was fuming mad, and smart enough to realize it, but too stupid to know why. She took the icon none-too-gently between her teeth, pulled it down, and carried it inside the cabin, where she dropped it on the old man's bed of stones with a clatter.

Then the clearing felt even emptier than before.

A fortnight came and went, and still Batiushka did not return. Joy grew so hungry, she ate all the vegetables in the garden—that is, the ones that the rabbits and birds hadn't stolen yet—and then hid in shame in her cave. But no one scolded her.

After a month she was painfully thin, and went fishing in the creek. It was the first flesh she'd eaten in a long time. The fish were small and difficult to catch, and it took hours to fill her stomach.

Most nights she dreamed she was in vigil with Batiushka. Sometimes he was an old man, face bright as the stars, and sometimes he was a young cub, the tips of his fur lit up by the moon. Always he gazed up at the icon lovingly.

Joy would try to call out to him, to tell him to watch out, to beware of the dark shadows lurking in the trees, but she had no voice.

When she woke from these dreams, she would run through the forests to the cabin to see if he had come back, and finding him gone, race down the path to the monastery and stand staring at the edge of the trees.

A hatred for the quiet buildings grew inside her. They stood with their backs to her, closing her out, she who had stood by the old man through the darkest moments. They had stolen him from her, the men who could not even lead their simple lives at the hermitage.

Worse, he had gone to them. He had left her and given himself to them, turned to them instead of Joy, who loved him most, who was most faithful. She had nearly

CHAPTER ELEVEN · 129

forgotten now how close he had been to death when she had helped him down the path. All she could think of was her hurt. Because he should have been back by now. He had chosen them over her.

And she was all alone again.

The great darkness was elsewhere doing other great mischief, and had no interest in only a bear, but Joy needed no demons to torment her from the outside now. The painful emptiness lived inside her.

Four months passed. Brown leaves dropped from the trees and soon were covered in snow. The creek froze over. Joy had no stores of fat to allow her to hibernate. She went to the edge of the wood and lay down in the snow, turning her eyes to the dome and cross that pricked the sun like a blackened needle.

She had taken him here. She had done it. She had followed him and helped him all the way here, after a thousand nights of darkness, and he had left her in the woods and gone on. And the Lady with stars, the Lady from the icon, the Joy of all Joys, yes, she had him now. She had taken him.

Joy did not understand any of it, and she was angry. The emptiness inside her was tearing her open. It was the darkness again, the emptiness, the despair, and she could not escape it now, because there was no Batiushka.

The sun set and the church bells rang, and she made no move to get up.

As she lay there, the sound of singing echoed from the wood, and a soft ray of golden light fell across her back. Joy lifted her head and looked behind her, and she saw a procession coming down the path.

It wound its way from some other part of the world—

or perhaps some other world entirely—led by babes barely old enough to walk, toddling on unsteady legs that somehow never fell. Their perfect hands waved banners of silver and sapphire; a hymn of joyful enthusiasm somehow united their voices. They passed Joy in the grass, and had she been a woman, she would have wept for the wanting of them.

Behind the babes walked young men and maidens, robed in white, with flowers in their hair and crosses on their breasts. A sweet perfume filled the air around them, and on their lips the song of the babes became sweet and solemn.

Following them was a great crowd of saints, of every nation and race, men and women such as Joy had never seen before, singing the hymn all in a single language of words that even the bear could understand.

> *Thou art a gold-entwined tower*
> *and twelve-walled encircled city!*
> *A throne besprinkled with sunbeams,*
> *a royal chair of the King!*
> *O inexplicable wonder,*
> *that Thou dost milk-feed the Master....*

Finally there came twelve men, with golden voices and faces too bright for Joy to look upon, and in the midst of them walked the Lady.

Joy knew her at once.

CHAPTER ELEVEN · 133

She had seen that face, both young and ancient, full of sorrow and joy, a thousand times on a thousand nights, when all else seemed bleak and hopeless. She had watched from the trees as the Lady took Batiushka away into the monastery. Suddenly Joy felt the enormous injustice of her own childlessness. She'd had only Batiushka in all her life, and now this Lady with a thousand children had stolen him away as well.

The Lady passed her by without a glance, her eyes fixed on the monastery ahead.

Joy felt a burning anger inside. She rose to her feet. When the last of the procession had gone by, she followed them toward the dwellings of men.

The golden domes and crosses rose high from the earth like fangs, piercing the sky, but the procession continued fearlessly. Joy's legs trembled, and the scent of men filled her nostrils. She had never sensed such danger all around her. She followed the others into the midst of the buildings and wondered that no one heard their singing or came running out to greet them. When they mounted the steps of a stone house four or even five times the size of Batiushka's cabin, the door swung open of its own accord, and blue-tinged flames flared in the unlit lamps inside. The procession entered, spilling into the building like a river into a jar. Joy couldn't see how everyone would fit. She would surely be left outside. Her heart pounded as her claws scratched the stone steps.

But there was no crowding, for the children led them down a passageway and into a tunnel where the ceiling turned from wood to rock. They passed through a maze of caves beneath the earth. Corridors branched away at each turn, leading to simple wooden doors shut fast against the night. If anyone was behind them, they must have slept very soundly not to hear the din of the children's voices, which grew more and more melancholy as they traveled deeper.

> *Thou art the sweetness of angels,*
> *the gladness of afflicted ones,*
> *and the Protectress of Christians,*
> *O Virgin Mother of our God!*

They turned a corner and found another closed door, but this one the procession walked straight through, the door parting for them like a curtain. Joy closed her eyes as she passed through the wood. When she opened them, only the Lady and two of the shining men remained of the procession, although the song went on.

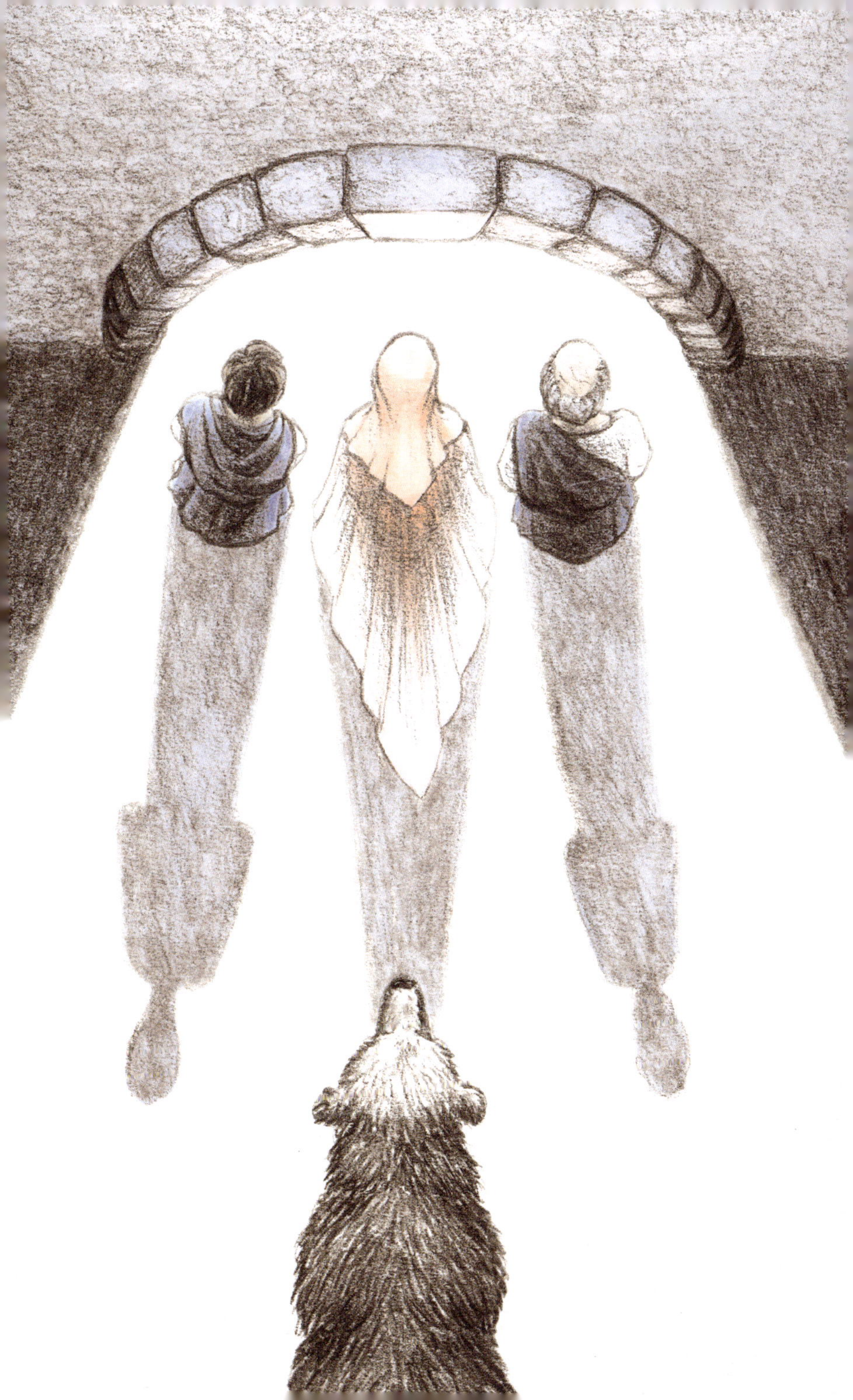

*Be Thou my helper and save me
from out of eternal torments...*

On a cot in the corner lay Batiushka, thin and transparent as a ghost, his silver hair gleaming in the light of the saints' faces. The rise and fall of his chest was barely visible.

Joy almost bounded to his side, but something moved on the opposite side of the room, and the bear crouched low and flattened her ears.

A younger man stood at a table, crushing powder with a mortar and pestle, and glancing every so often at a page in an open book by his side. Metal instruments and piles of bandages lay in a mess on the table around him, and he looked nervous. He seemed not to notice the intruders at all.

The Lady glided forward. She stretched out a hand and touched Batiushka's cheek. Her skin shone golden brown and luminous against his porcelain face, and Joy was somehow afraid it would shatter him, but he opened his eyes at her touch.

His lips moved. *My Joy.*

Joy could not bear it. She turned to run from the room, but the closed door was behind her, and this time

CHAPTER ELEVEN · 137

it would not let her pass. She turned back around, ears drooping.

The Lady looked to her two companions. "He is one of ours," she said. Her face shone, and so did those of the two men, brighter and brighter until Joy could see nothing but light all around, such light that she cowered by the door and covered her eyes with her paws. She couldn't stand it.

The blinding light seemed to last an eternity. She thought it would never end.

And then she found she could open her eyes again, and the room under the earth was gone. Batiushka was gone. She was back in the clearing, on the rock in front of the tree, and the Lady stood in front of her, still more radiant than the moon. For the first time that night, the Lady looked directly into her eyes, and Joy trembled. She was terrified, but the anger, the darkness, the emptiness was still inside her, eating her up, and she could have screamed at the thief in front of her had she any words.

The Joy of all Joys raised her hand.

The forest around them fell like a curtain from some invisible rod. They were motionless, the Lady, the rock,

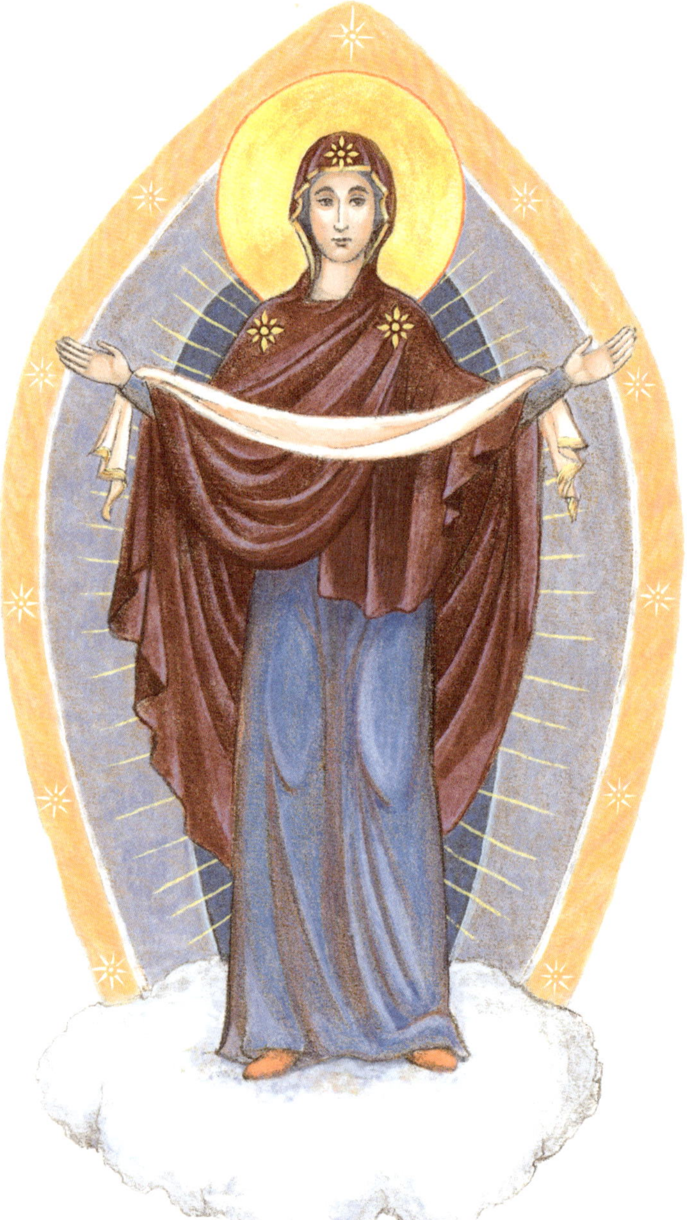

and the bear, as unfamiliar scenes revolved above, below, and around them.

Joy could no longer tell which way was up and which was down. She gripped the rock with her claws, terrified she would fall.

The images filled her vision. A young boy was falling from a great height, flailing desperately with his arms and legs to catch hold of something. There was the Lady, stepping out of a church below and raising her arms to the sky in supplication. Invisible hands slowed the child's descent, curled his jerking body into a ball, and rolled him gently to the ground.

A weeping woman stumbled out of her house, carrying the same boy, whose blue eyes were bright with fever. The crowd parted for them as a procession came down the street, bearing an icon of the Lady and her Child. "Kiss her, pray to her," the woman whispered urgently in the boy's ear, and he obeyed, putting fingers to chapped lips and reaching to touch the icon's gilt border as it passed by.

The boy was a man now, his long nose and wispy hair familiar. He lay deathly ill in bed, legs swollen, eyes clenched shut against the pain. The Lady appeared, her two companions with her, and touched his hand. His eyes opened, and indescribable joy filled his face as she said the words, "He is one of ours."

Scene after scene flashed by, and Joy saw him grow, saw him pray, saw him stand rapt before visions no others could see. She felt the warmth and fullness flooding through him. And always the Lady stood, beside him and before him, her hands outstretched to heaven.

And then she saw a cabin in the woods, and everything in nature served the man. The bee gave its honey, the bird its song, the sun its light, and the earth its fruits. Only one creature took from him constantly.

A dark bear, sad-eyed, like an endless chasm, soaking up every bit of attention and love.

Constantly bringing her darkness to him, like a never-ending night.

Lashing out with harsh winds of jealousy and resentment.

Draining his energies with her own weariness and despair.

And of all the bright and beautiful creatures that came to the woods, this one monster did the Lady give the man as a constant companion. It seemed more like a curse than a gift.

Death is my name, thought the bear.

The scenes faded, and the forest slowly rose again around them.

Joy turned her eyes to the Lady. Their dark depths seemed to reach out, pleading for something.

The Lady touched the bear's snout.

"Why?" Joy asked. It was the only word she ever said.

"For the fullness of Joy," came the answer.

The beautiful face brightened and grew still, and was only an icon swaying from the branch of the tree.

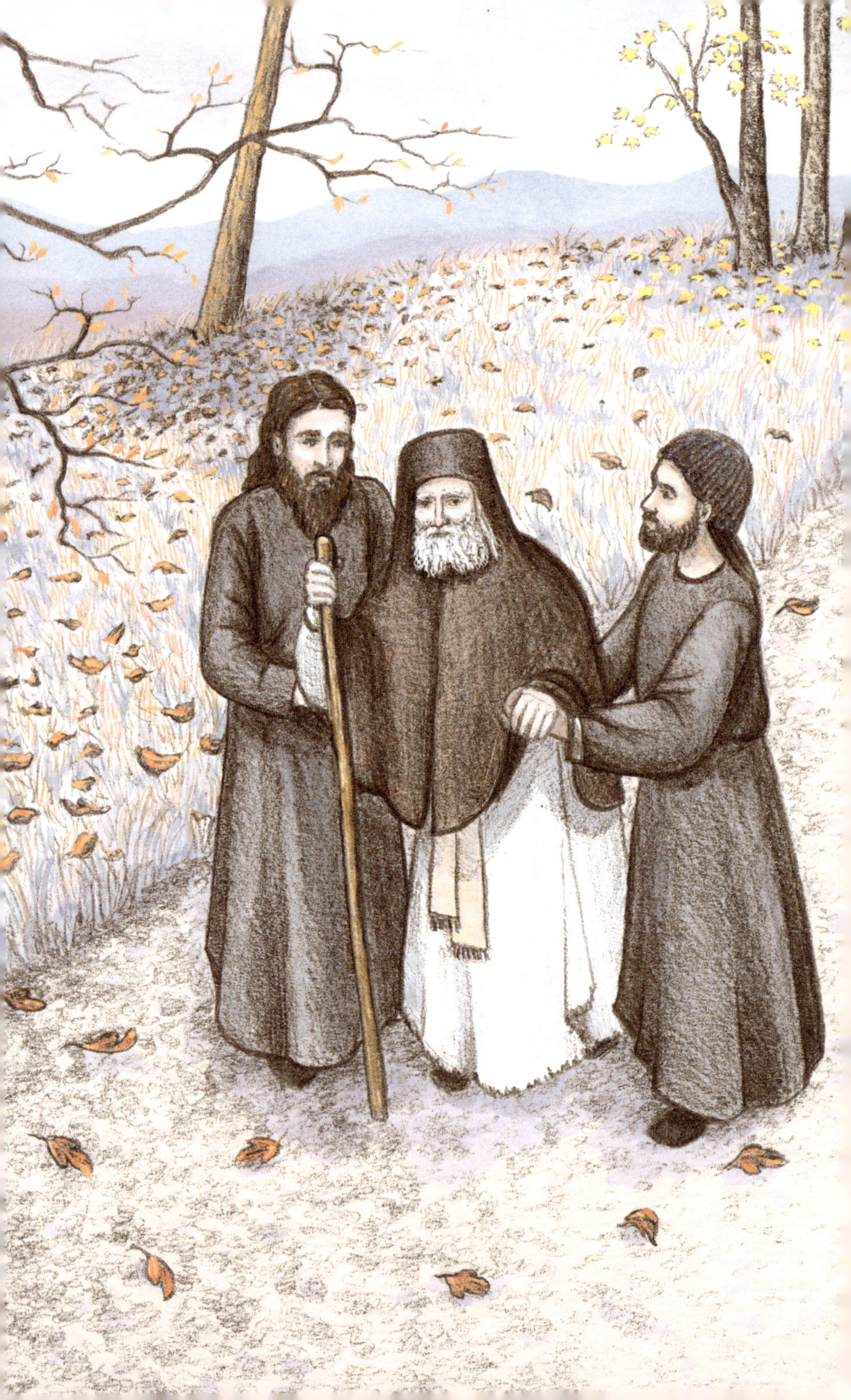

CHAPTER TWELVE

He returned one day when the morning sun could barely melt the icy frost from the oak leaves on the ground.

Joy was waiting for him at the start of the path, and rose to her feet slowly when she saw the little group approaching. She felt oddly sad to see him, although she had been waiting months for nothing else. She wondered if he might read everything that had happened in her face.

Batiushka shuffled along with the help of a cane, and the two novices with him held their hands out nervously with his every wobble, clearly afraid he would fall. His hair had turned white in the months he was gone.

Joy was not bothered by the other men now. She moved forward to put her head against Batiushka's chest. He smelled of incense and roses—of the Lady. And this no longer bothered her either.

Misunderstanding, the old man patted her shoulder and drew a piece of bread from his pocket.

It was not what Joy had wanted, but she didn't let it go to waste.

"You are an old creature like me now," he said, running his fingers through the white hairs in her muzzle. He looked deep in her cloudy brown eyes. There was something different about them.

She chuffed at him and put her head to his chest again.

He rubbed her shoulder fondly, and his hands still had strength in them. "Only one more parting, I promise," he said.

They walked back to the cabin together. Joy and Batiushka took the lead. They walked very slowly for the old man's sake, but even so, the two younger monks walked several paces behind, cautiously watching the bear.

"You're sure we cannot do anything for you, Batiushka?" they asked when they had reached the clearing. "Fetch some firewood? Draw water?"

CHAPTER TWELVE · 145

He shooed them away. "Go, go, don't worry about me," he said cheerfully. "You've brought enough food for me to live on for a year! And I have my Joy."

The two bags they left were full of bread, vegetables, grain, preserves, sugar, salt, and tea. Joy's mouth watered as Batiushka unpacked them and stacked everything carefully against the cabin wall, where the bags of dirt had once been. She was glad to see the provisions, since she had eaten everything in the garden by now.

The young men kissed Batiushka's hand and hugged him tightly before leaving. When they had gone, he sighed and sat down on the porch.

Joy sat next to him.

There was a long, beautiful silence, as in the old days. A few birds flew down from the trees to eat the crumbs he scattered, and a cat Joy had never seen before came trotting out of the woods to sit at the old man's feet.

"We have been stricken with many trials now, my Joy," he said finally. "I think it is time for a little quiet."

Quiet he was. The beautiful silence continued, through their chores, through prayers, and into the night. He worked silently, prayed silently, and kissed Joy's nose in silence before going to bed.

She thought little of the change, even the next day when the silence stretched on. They had never needed words, anyway. She could feel the prayer turning constantly in his heart,

> *Gospodi Iisuse Khriste, Syne Bozhiy,*
> *pomiluy mya greshnago.*

Joy's heart, which was finally timid and quiet, echoed it back to him. She stayed close at all times, sleeping on the porch instead of in her den.

Winter came before either of them were really ready. Not just in the woods, where the snow fell thick and fast, but in Joy, whose joints were stiff and whose fur was speckled with silver and white. She sensed that she was near the end of her life, and in the ancient wisdom of beasts, she did not mourn.

Batiushka fed her from his hands and brought her indoors when she had trouble standing after a night in the cold. He never spoke aloud, but when he turned to the icon of the Lady, Joy would come join him, and when he opened the cabin door for her, she would go off a ways into the snow to do her business. They understood each other perfectly.

It was what Joy had always wanted. But she saw now

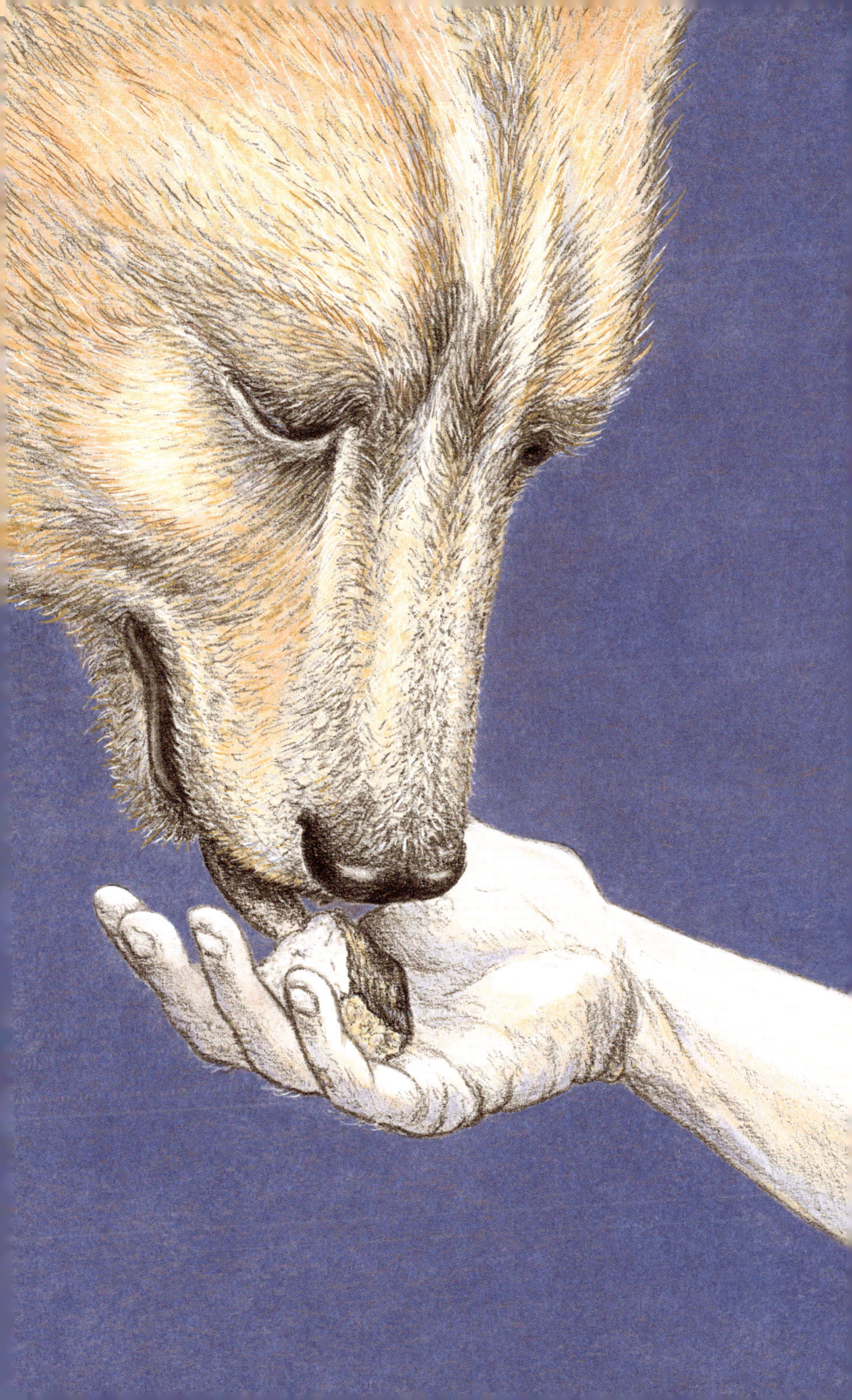

that she didn't deserve it. When the Lady looked at them through the icon, Joy could feel the darkness of all her life next to the brightness of Batiushka's, and she was ashamed.

That was the only sadness of old age. That her chance to repay him for all she had taken was gone. Some days she went out and looked toward the trees, wondering if she should wander off like Misha and free the old man from her burdensome presence.

But every time she felt him calling her back, and she obeyed.

One day when the snows had barely melted, a monk came to the cabin and talked for a long time to Batiushka.

"The new abbot says you must return, Father. He says it is not right that you stay out here alone. You don't come to services, you don't partake of Holy Communion—he says it's not good for you."

Batiushka sat on the porch and listened silently.

"He worries for you, Batiushka. He knows you need the fellowship of your brothers."

Silence.

"It is not setting a good example for the novices."

CHAPTER TWELVE · 149

Silence.

"If he allows you to do as you wish, how will he say no to others?"

The longer Batiushka was silent, the more the monk talked and fidgeted. When he could think of nothing else to say, he held out his hand and looked at Batiushka for a long time. When the old man just looked back at him, the monk finally dropped his hand and left.

Batiushka came inside to Joy, who had listened to the one-sided exchange. He fed her a piece of bread, and went to stand in front of the prayer corner. She joined him.

He wept again that day, as he had so long ago on the bench in Gethsemane. Afterward, he sat down with Joy in front of the fire, and rested with his hand on her head.

It is almost the end.

She could feel him think it, and knew he was right.

Every end of one season is the beginning of another.

She knew he was right in this, too. She thought of water roaring and fish leaping in the great rivers. Of cubs tumbling in the new grass and flowers opening toward the sun. She thought of a long night of vigil ending, and the sun rising pink in the east.

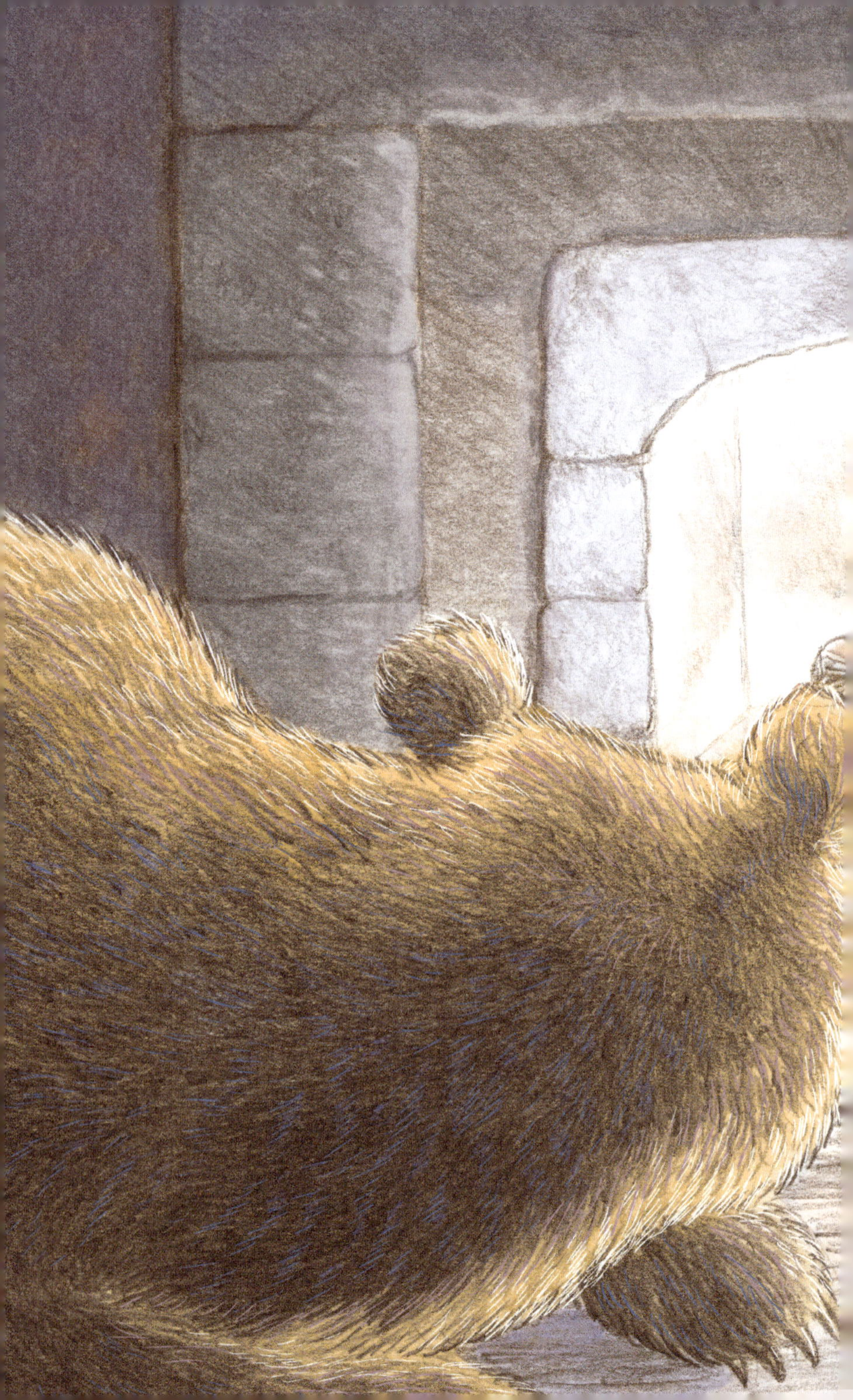

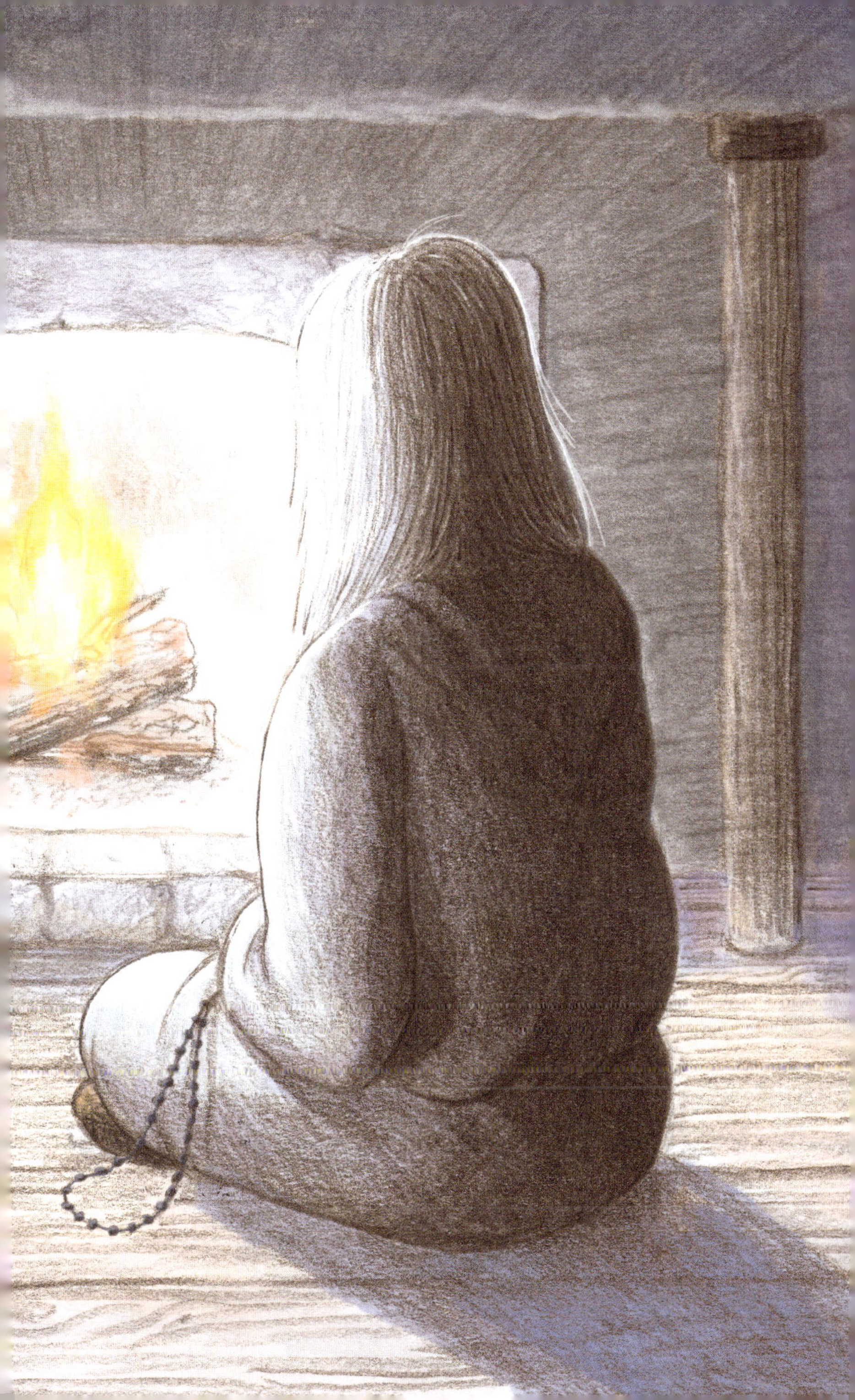

THE FULLNESS OF JOY

He patted her gently and gave her more bread.

A week later, another monk came with an official-looking letter. Batiushka did not read it, just put it in his pocket and took his cane from the corner. He carefully picked up the icon of the Lady from the prayer corner, then gave Joy one last kiss on the head as a goodbye.

CHAPTER TWELVE · 153

She stood on the porch and watched him hobble away down the path. Even when he was out of sight, she could hear the prayer turning around and around in his heart.

Gospodi Iisuse Khriste, Syne Bozhiy,
pomiluy mya greshnago.

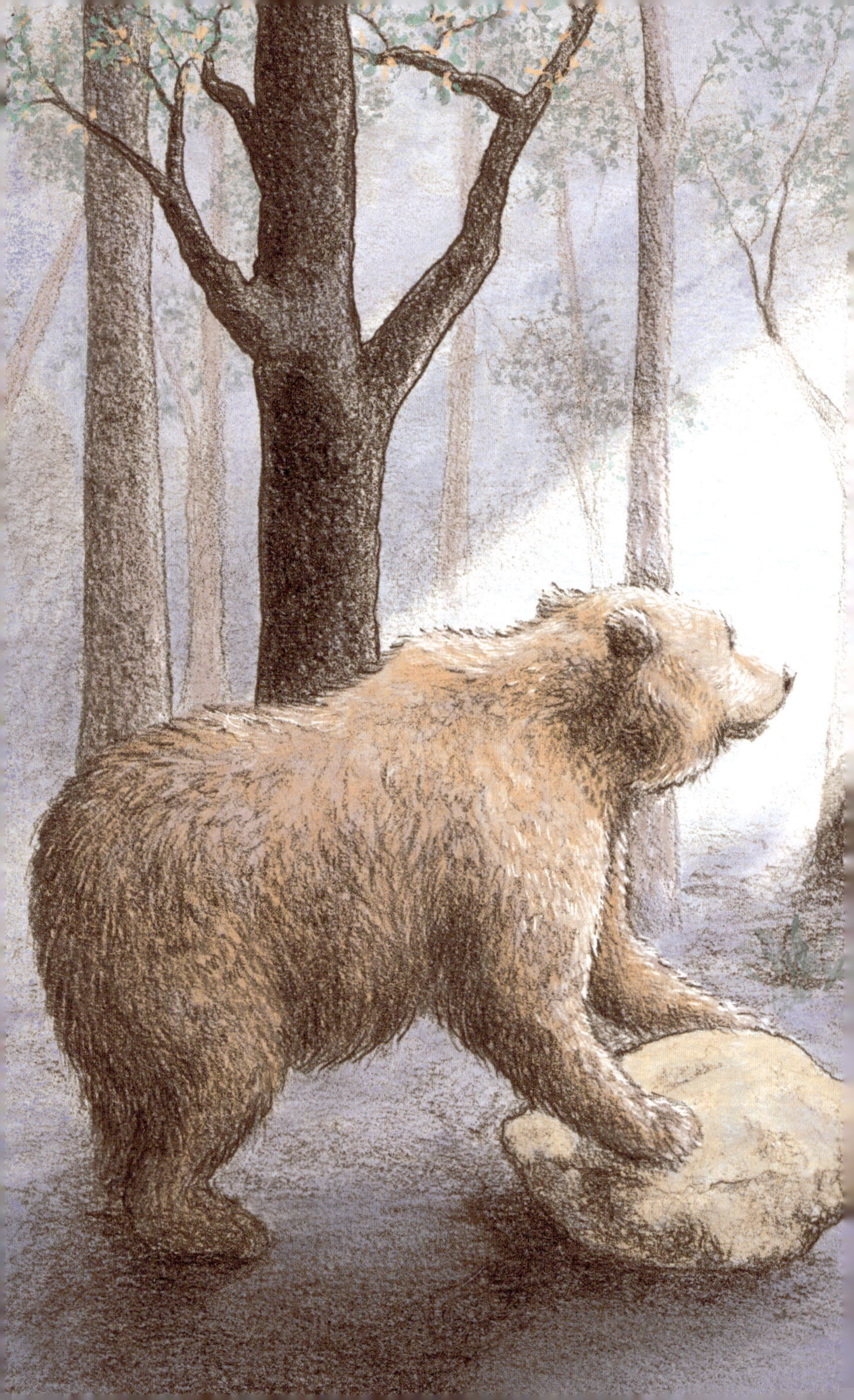

The sun set, and Joy limped through sprigs of new grass to the rock in the clearing. She climbed slowly up and stood, cold paws on cold rock, as the moon rose.

She was only a bear, and she had no words, but she looked up to the stars, and in her eyes were all the sights the Lady had shown her. She laid out her great darkness before the Great Light she knew was somewhere in the heavens above.

She was only a bear, but if she were a woman, she might have said,

I am Death, but I am yours now, Master.

And if she were a woman, clever and proud, she might not have heard the answer,

I have touched Death itself, and all that I touch turns to Joy.

AUTHOR'S NOTE

This book is based on the very real story of Saint Seraphim of Sarov, a great staretz, or spiritual elder, of Russia in the nineteenth century. My primary source for details of the saint's life was the biography, *Saint Seraphim of Sarov* by Valentine Zander, which is a perfect starting point for anyone interested in learning more about the saint. I would not presume to write the thoughts of Saint Seraphim himself, so instead I have imagined how things might have been for one of the creatures who came to him in his cabin in the woods. His most well-known bear, Misha, shows up in many stories and icons, but Joy is only a bear who might have been. Joy is me. Joy is you, reader.

In this I am afraid I have taken a few creative liberties, such as imagining how life was with Saint Seraphim during his period as a recluse, and placing Joy as a witness in several important events. In this I pray I have

AUTHOR'S NOTE

not gone too far, but overall given a faithful impression of what Saint Seraphim was like.

The most dramatic aspects of the story—Saint Seraphim's thousand nights of prayer, his near-death at the hands of robbers, and his miraculous healing vision of the Mother of God with the disciples Saint Peter and Saint John—are all taken from his original biography. Accounts differ in some minor aspects of the timeline, so I've done my best to follow Zander's biography, which is not always specific about the order of events. The geography of Sarov Monastery and the hermitage in the woods was also difficult to research due to Sarov's current state as one of Russia's nuclear testing facilities, closed to the general public. There are doubtless some small discrepancies as to the proximity of the praying rock to the cabin, the layout of the path, and other details, but again, I pray I have overall given a faithful impression.

We end this volume with Batiushka Seraphim's words of greeting to everyone he met:

"Christ is Risen, my joy!"

GEORGIA BRIGGS is an Alabama native who has loved drawing and writing since childhood. As an adult she converted to Eastern Orthodoxy, where she found the fulfillment of the beauty and mystery she had always longed for. Georgia is now a mother, iconographer, and the author of the award-winning novel *Icon*.